THE STING OF
DEATH

THE STING OF DEATH

JESSICA MANN

PUBLISHED FOR THE CRIME CLUB BY
DOUBLEDAY & COMPANY, INC.
GARDEN CITY, NEW YORK
1983

All of the characters in this book
are fictitious, and any resemblance
to actual persons, living or dead,
is purely coincidental.

Library of Congress Cataloging in Publication Data

Mann, Jessica.
The sting of death.

I. Title.
PR6063.A374S7   1983   823'.914
ISBN 0-385-18701-7
Library of Congress Catalog Card Number 82-45868

THE STING OF
DEATH

PROLOGUE

The girl had not driven the car before, but she knew which controls to operate. Her subconscious mind had been preparing for flight long before she went.

She steered down the mountainside, gripping hard to the wheel, leaning forward to peer through the smeared windscreen. Invisible death waited round the bends in the road. Gaps in the clouds showed rivers and fields far below. Almost more terrifying were the patches of grey nothingness against the window and the sudden revelation, inches ahead, of pebble-scattered corners.

She tried repeatedly to concentrate on the unfamiliar task of driving. But images of terror superimposed themselves upon her mind, as they had since the baby was born: of fires and falls, disease and disaster—and, now, the fear of pursuit.

But she had left the others marooned when she took the little car, behind which the caravan had been towed. They must still be there, in a stoned, unsavoury stupor. She thought of the black-tipped fingers brushing against her baby's cheek, holding the smoke to his lips. "There you are, mate. You try it."

"Not for him!" She had snatched him up against her.

"Why not? Got to get the right start in life."

She was frightened of the others now, as of so much else. She looked at their mocking, hostile faces and sat very still, pressing the warm, damp bundle against her, and waited while they laughed, and yawned, and put the thought of her away until the next time.

Eventually they were all asleep. She disentangled her skirt from a grey foot which poked through a torn canvas shoe, and eased herself up as gently as a spillikin. The baby stirred, but quietly, and she made no noise as she took the shaggy coat and the lumpy sleeping bag—both matted with dirt—and, from the drawer under the bunk, the package of money.

It was dark night when she left. She felt nothing as she looked, before closing the trailer's door, at the child's father; nothing, as she drove away, but resolution and fear, fear and resolution. The mountains were hardly emerging from winter. She had wanted her child's nature to awake, and her own to reawaken, to spring.

There was more money than she had expected: a dowry. The girl bought food, and clean wrappings for her son, and fuel for the car. She could have afforded to stop now, but passed by the resort villages and spa towns. She sensed the chase behind her as she pressed on through hills and across plains, over rivers swollen with meltwater and mountain passes still banked with the shovelled snow of the previous autumn, and so to the gentler west, where the dipping, swelling fields were green and the clean houses with their russet shutters tempted her to stay.

But she wanted to put the Channel between them.

It was dusk when she came to a fishing village. The fleet was putting out to sea, lamps sparkling from the mastheads. Nets lay spread or heaped on the stone blocks. Old men smoked and spat against the wall. The boats, which were at moorings, or keeled over on the beach, were covered with tarpaulins against the Atlantic.

The white yacht was tied along the quayside. The tide was half out, and the deck a long drop below where the girl stood. The owner was polishing brass on the wheelhouse. He looked up and said, "Hi."

She sat down, dangling her legs over the quay and clutching the cradle's handle. "Hi," she replied. "Are you going back to England?"

And he answered, "Welcome aboard."

CHAPTER 1

James came to the top of the dunes and over the brow of
the hill, and saw the tents in the field below; he stood suddenly still, so that Tamsin stepped against his heels. They
heard the voices of angry people coming from the encamp-
ment.

"Over my dead body," they heard. "I simply won't have
it. You knew perfectly well . . ."

James said, "That's my cousin Simon's voice."

"You knew what you were getting yourself into," a
deeper male voice said.

"No, I hadn't any idea it would be like this. You'd no
right to use my place . . . When I found those things I—"

" 'Rights' yet!" said another voice.

"It was never part of the agreement," Simon grumbled.

"So what are you going to do about it?" the first man
asked. "Call the police?"

A girl laughed, and a man whose native language was
evidently not English said, "You wanted the money. And
we've paid, haven't we?"

"Yes, but that was just for . . . You can't have thought I
wanted to be involved in anything else."

The camp was in the field nearest the orchard, where
Granny Wherry's donkeys had lived.

Beyond the heavy-blossomed orchard was the farmhouse,
a small, low building, set in a hollow because protection
from the weather mattered more than a long view in the
sixteenth century.

The fields nearest the house were once the most profitable on the whole farm. Now they were degraded by two
years of neglect. Simon, Granny's heir, neither cultivated

them himself, nor would let them to his neighbour, Leonard Hosking. And how he had turned the fertile land over to the twentieth century's crop: campers, holidaymakers, tourists.

"Not at Grebe," James said aloud. "I won't have it here." Grebe was sacred: the land for its natural properties, the sea for its mystery, the beach for its treasures and the nitrogen-bearing seaweed.

Today Tamsin Oriel had accompanied James on his regular walk round the headland. He carried a polythene sack and put other people's litter into it: sandwich papers, sweet packets, bottles and cans which had held chemical drinks. James hardly classified the litter anymore, after two years of performing his self-imposed chore. At first he used to make fanciful deductions, postulating cheerful family parties, and adventurous children chewing toffee as they explored the woods. He would attribute emotions to the users of the rubber contraceptives, and found their detritus in some way less deplorable, as an affirmation of the life force.

The path rose away from the river, and followed the line of the cliff which bounded the southern side of the Grebe peninsula. Stretching eastwards, the pleated cliffs rose from the sea.

As they walked along the path, Tamsin had listened to James talking about his children and the future they would have in this happy environment, safe from the corruptions of towns and machines, intimately involved with nature and primary food production.

At the end of the cliff path, they had gone down to cross the beach, past a noisy, alien gang who were cooking meat on a fire set in a circle of pebbles, and fell silent as Tamsin and James drew close. A burst of laughter followed when they turned into the sand dunes.

James had once experienced a unique rapture here. He had been reading poetry in the hollow between two great mounds of sand, lulled to pleasure by the sensuous words and the sounds of a midsummer day, when a mild sea was far out on the beach below, and rabbits came out of their burrows beside him, and birds settled on the ground nearby. He raised his eyes from the drowsy verse, and saw what in another mood he would have found incredible.

The wings' perfect blue, their ebony tips, the perfection of the shape of the butterfly dazzled him, and left its image printed on his memory as it fluttered out of sight. No collector's pleasure this, for he would have killed himself as soon as the insect; nor a publicity-seeker's, for he took a solitary joy in what he had seen.

The impulse faded as soon as it was formulated, to announce that he had seen at Grebe an example of a species which had almost died out in the British Isles. He knew the price which butterflies fetched from conscienceless collectors.

James visited the professor of biology in his hometown at the beginning of the next term, and was sent on to the centre where such sightings were recorded. He had been interrogated about the accuracy of his memory and the innocence of his intention like a witness in a murder trial, but at last it was noted on a printed card that a Large Blue Butterfly had been sighted by James Buxton at Grebe, and when, and in what circumstances; and James watched as the card was put into an envelope which was then sealed with red wax and signet rings in several places, and marked with prohibitions about opening, before it was stored in a filing cabinet. It was explained that by doing this the information would not be revealed to any researcher who was working through the files. All that the world might know was that somewhere unspecified, in southwest England, an example of this threatened species had been seen. James was made happier by the memory of that portentous moment than he would have been by any album full of newspaper clippings about his discovery.

He had never seen another Large Blue. But the aura of excitement and joy still pervaded the sand dunes at Grebe. He intended that his ashes should be scattered there one day.

As he and Tamsin walked along the path, James glanced about at the familiar features of the dunes. In one hollow he found the traces of another fire and carefully buried the fragments of cooking foil and the empty beer cans which lay around it.

"They must know how dangerous it is to light fires here," he said bitterly. "Yes, really dangerous. The fire could spread underground along the roots of the grass."

"I don't suppose they have much thought for the morrow," Tamsin said.

"Not many people do. Instant pleasure, instant money, instant fulfilment. Don't you think the world has taken a wrong turn?" He wondered what such people would understand of his craftsman's satisfaction in putting wood aside to season, and shaping it, after a wait of months or years, into something which future generations would enjoy. What would they make of the idea of planting the seeds of trees which would give shade to their descendants?

"I suppose it's natural to want things now, not later," Tamsin admitted.

"If we grab them now, there won't be a later. The world won't survive our depredations."

The edge of the dunes was bounded by a wall, a core of stone covered with earth and grass to form a smoothly curved bank. On the other side of the boundary Leonard Hosking's fields were green with pushing shoots of barley.

And at that point James and Tamsin saw below them the scrubby, neglected fields of Grebe, wasted land, with their new, bitter crop of tents.

James shrugged impatiently, without interest or understanding, at the conversation which he could hear coming from them. He started down the slope.

The first tent they came to was open and empty, its fly sheet flapping in the breeze. James glanced in and saw some books and papers on an upturned orange box, weighted against the wind by a bottle of whisky and by a wide-necked jar which contained— No! The protest screamed through James's mind.

In the jar, motionless in death, was a butterfly. Its azure wings were dimmed, but the black wingtips shone like jet in the poisoned cell.

This is how it feels to have a heart attack, James thought.

His heart thumped like a piston-driven engine. He felt sick. His eyes were veiled by a pink haze. He crouched on the ground gasping, and then put his head down between his knees. Many times in his life James had been tormented by humanity's wanton blindness. He had agonised over the disposal of nuclear waste, over the destruction of the atmosphere by hydrocarbon-fuel emissions, over the squandering of irreplaceable natural resources. He had the certainty of a religious fanatic backed by proof. His truth was evident; it did not pass all understanding. Often James felt the frustration which must have been the fate of the prophets. He was a Cassandra, warning of avoidable disaster, but speaking to deaf ears.

The dead Large Blue Butterfly symbolised the wicked folly of the world. James unscrewed the lid of the jar and tipped the butterfly onto his palm. It felt like a piece of paper, as light and meaningless as an old shopping list. Its colour, undimmed in death, matched the sky.

The life cycle of the Large Blue Butterfly was dependent on the coincidence of a particular variety of ant, and of a certain wild thyme, both rare separately, and more rare together. If the butterflies were netted to make a fast buck, the species, once known in eight counties of southern England, was certainly doomed.

James wrapped the butterfly in his handkerchief and put it gently in his pocket. Tamsin looked relieved when he got up. He thought, but did not care, that she probably supposed he was mad. He shouted, "Simon!"

The quarrelling voices instantly fell silent. They had been muttering, inaudibly to Tamsin, unattended by James. After a moment, Simon's voice said, "That's my cousin. You stay here, I'll . . ." He came out from a green bell-tent, bending under the flap of canvas. "Hullo, James," he said, unsmiling. "Oh, Tamsin. You here too? What do you—? Oh well, never mind. This isn't a very good moment, as it happens."

Tamsin blushed. Simon hardly looked at her, and she walked on, across the field and through the orchard. She stepped aside to avoid a torn hammock, still hanging where

it had been slung years before; past a heap of stones where
Simon and James had once buried a dog; past a beehive,
disused since Simon proved allergic to bee stings; through
the broken gate, dangling from one rusty hinge; and she
waited out of earshot, beside the overgrown garden wall. A
smell of paraffin and bottled gas came from the open door
of the house, to mingle with the sweet scented shrubs.

James squared his shoulders. He had spent many years
quarrelling, losing quarrels, and patching them up again,
with his cousin Simon.

"Those tents," he exclaimed. "You know damn well you
aren't allowed—" Simon stared at him. James went on, more
quietly, "I shall report you. You can't . . ."

Simon started to reply in a similar manner, and stopped,
and drew a deep breath. His face was pale, so that his
freckles stood out against a white background. His reddish
hair was long and dirty, and he smelt of whisky and old
sweat.

"James, old man," Simon said in a controlled voice. He
dropped his arm round James's shoulder, and the matted
wool of his fisherman's jersey scratched briefly against
James's cheek. "I think," he went on, propelling his cousin
down the hill, away from the tents, "I don't want you to
come to Grebe for the time being. After all, it does belong
to me. I could say you were trespassing. Okay?"

"Not—not come to Grebe?"

"Damn it," Simon cried, his voice high, as though he
were suddenly losing a mannerly restraint. "After all, damn
it, you do nothing but criticise. Why don't I dig this, prune
that, Granny would be sad to see the other, make it good
here, cut it down there, mend a fence, dig a ditch—all your
little schemes, one after another, you produce them as solu-
tions to problems you'll never understand. I didn't specially
want Grebe, but now I've got it I'll keep it the way I
bloody well like. And if I want to let people camp here I
will. If I choose to have a bloody pop festival, who's to stop
me? It's mine—mine—not yours. Mine as long as I live. So
shove off, James, go home to your hens and woodwork and
your pious self-sufficiency. Granny left Grebe to me be-

cause I was the son of her eldest son. And I daresay she knew what a wet you were. So go home, Jimmy boy. Go back home."

Simon walked over to Tamsin. His face, though still pale, was now a polite mask, the face of the diplomat he had once thought of becoming, before he inherited his tiny estate, and before his ambitious father died and deprived him of moral propulsion; before he began to drink a bottle of whisky a day. "Good of you to call," he said formally.

Tamsin glanced up at his face. "Simon, I—"

"I'm so sorry. You'll think I'm simply too inhospitable for words. I do hope so very much that you'll forgive me. But I'm dreadfully tied up just at the minute. I think I'm going to be incommunicado for a while. I fear I shan't be able to invite you to Grebe at present. Of course you're always free to walk on the public footpaths; it's lovely by the river at this time of year. But if you would—you and my cousin too —perhaps you'd better just go off now. Go home, why don't you? Just go home."

CHAPTER 2

Anna saw at once that James was upset. She watched him through the window as he came up the drive, his lips moving as though he were repeating some phrase, and his hands clenching and opening.

She jerked her attention back to the critic from the local paper who had been asking stupid questions about Ivory Judd's private life, instead of studying her work.

"Do say something about her new approach to the landscape," Anna urged. "It's such a significant advance when you see it in context. Compare the downs over there with this new painting of Penwith—look, in 'Winter Mystery Two.'"

"God knows why she gives those fancy names to her pictures," the young man muttered. "Though I'll admit the mystery part in this one."

Anna always expected to enjoy the private-view parties she gave for each new exhibition. The preceding days, if hectic, were happy, with everyone sharing the common aim and enthusiasm while hanging and rearranging the exhibits. Eighteen months' experience had not yet taught her that the show would not be a sellout on the first day; that the reviewers, no matter what they said as they drank her wine and ground their cigarettes into her floor, would "think with both hands for a fortnight" to find a crabby comment, rather than write undiluted praise. They seemed to suppose that readers would scorn them for being corrupt or credulous if they actually admitted that a collection of artists' work was marvellous. Little did they realise, and as little did Anna remember, at that stage, that nobody will ever seem to have read a review of anyone else's work.

Sometimes Anna would pin cuttings above her desk, if they were even half-flattering, in the hope of priming the pump of praise. Visitors who had bought the paper from which they were clipped every day of their adult lives would deny having seen them before. "Darling, how super," they would say. "However did I miss it? Perhaps it was left out of our edition."

Ivory Judd was not one of those painters who skulked in the stockroom whilst the invited guests crammed in to see her work. She circulated busily, making a point of introducing herself all around. In fact, it would have been hard for any visitor who had glanced at the pictures on the wall not to recognise Ivory Judd.

Ivory's landscapes appealed strongly to Anna's taste. They were subtle in design and colour, and she captured in paint what Anna appreciated in the countryside. Her human portraits, on the other hand, were slabs of harsh colour and angles; invariably of naked bodies, often of her own, and oddly, since they were not intended to be quite naturalistic, instantly recognisable.

Some of James's work was also on show; two chairs made of yew wood, a table in elm, a chest in walnut. Anna wondered whether he would pull himself together and come up from the workshop. It was not easy to find buyers for his work.

The room was crowded. The butcher, the baker, the candlestick-maker, Anna thought, looking round the room. But the butcher had splashed out on a Walter Wicks lithograph last Christmas; and the baker, who was on the local council, had been very helpful when she was applying for permission to convert the barn into a workshop and gallery.

"I wanted to enquire about that bureau," a voice said in her ear. Anna switched her attention back to duty.

"I am sorry," she said. "I was wondering where my little boy had got to. Yes, the bureau is a lovely piece, isn't it?"

"How much are you asking?" The speaker was a thin woman, probably in her forties, with tight white jeans stretched over wiry legs. She was a weekender from the other side of the county. On Friday evenings she and her family arrived with cases of provisions and rowed over to their motor cruiser. Anna could not remember when the boat had last been untied from the mooring. If it rained, the family returned at once to home comforts; but when the sun shone they spent the weekend lying on the cabin roof, drinking, and listening to the radio. Anna scorned, lest she should envy, their way of life. She mentioned the price of the bureau without needing to look it up. The woman gasped.

"But that's as much as an antique! Why, I could get a really good piece of furniture for that amount of money."

"The raw materials are very expensive," Anna recited, too accustomed to similar conversations to lose her temper. "And the whole thing is made by hand. It takes a great many man-hours, you know."

"All the same . . ." The woman went off to her husband's side, and Anna could see her thin brown hand, with several bangles on the wrist, gesticulating as she spoke. He was also wearing white trousers, with a rust-coloured canvas smock.

An occasion of this kind was a good opportunity to see the types of people who lived in, or regularly came to, south Cornwall. At Anna's private-view parties, guests came wearing their personal badges: the holidaymakers, rich and uncultured, who wore what they thought they would wear if they were poor and cultured; the painters whose clothes they were imitating, also in canvas trousers and smocks, but old and dirty ones, unadorned by gold jewellery and initialled belts. The bourgeoisie of Withiel adhered to the rule of dressing tidily for public occasions. Councillor Mrs. Lumb and her husband the Coroner were equally tightly corseted, and their tweed suits were alike in bulk and bulges. James and Anna's friends, other young couples who had moved away from big towns to live simple and natural lives, wore simple and natural clothes; their hair was simply and naturally uncut, and their simple, soft faces were naturally without makeup, because hours of work in the open air produced what, when they worked in offices, rouge had imitated. All were making statements about themselves: "I am Mrs. Lumb the Councillor, who does good to my community"; and, "I am Mr. Garage Proprietor, who can afford weekends on a motor cruiser and to wear a gold watch with sailing clothes"; and, "I am an artist—my mind is on higher things than personal adornment"; and, "I have chosen a life divorced from industry and artifice, and animals are not killed to make my shoes."

Perhaps the only two quite unselfconscious people in the room were Billy Buxton, aged not quite three, making himself sick on potato crisps in the corner of the room, and old Leonard Hosking from Grebe Vean Farm, Granny Wherry's neighbour. He had come to the party dressed as the older farmers did for Sunday chapel, in a shiny dark suit and a shirt with a separate collar, his red jowls swelling over its starched rim. He carried a hard hat in his hand, and had marched around the room with a certain doggedness to look at the pictures, his face as impassive as if he were bidding for a prizewinning cow in Truro market. His name was on the mailing list because he had bought one of James's chairs, some months ago, to present to Brannell Centenary Methodist Chapel in memory of his wife. Ever since, Mr. Hosking had accepted all the gallery's invitations; refused any alcoholic drink; refused the soft substitutes because, he said, "You never know what's in them things"; radiated disapproval and bafflement; and become an eccentric but lovable part of the gallery's attractions in the minds of the artists, who usually met people like Mr. Hosking only when they had put their easels in the wrong part of a field of standing corn.

Mr. Hosking had not much patience with most of the young, but James and Anna were forgiven, if not understood, for Granny's sake. He was less forebearing about Simon, who was not merely eccentric, but caused far more trouble and was mean about the grazing on Grebe.

"Here, Anna, you come along with me a minute." He grasped her arm and tugged her out onto the landing. He was shorter than she was, but his personality was powerful. He peered up into her face, and she sadly noticed the tight purple cheeks and watering eyes, signs of a lifetime's diet of Cornish cream and home-killed beef. He had been in hospital with heart attacks twice before Granny died, and often said that he'd never expected to attend her funeral.

"What's young Simon up to, then?" he asked, wheezing a little, but not loosening his grip on Anna's arm. "What's going on over to Grebe?"

"I don't know, Mr. Hosking. What do you mean?"

"Those friends of Simon's, if friends they are. Fine old rows they have together, as I can hear. Weird, un-Christian-looking folk. Maniacs on the road too. One of them knocked his wing mirror against a heifer and broke it off—his fault, edging up close to the cattle and roaring the motor. What did he expect? He panicked them."

"Oh dear," Anna said sympathetically.

"Don't know when I've heard such language. Heathen, it was, Anna, heathen. 'Take shame,' I told him. 'You wouldn't want for your Maker to hear such talk.' He looked proper dangerous; but there's no hurrying the animals, and so I told him."

"Who was it, Mr. Hosking?"

"Isn't that just what I'm asking you? Some foreigner, cluttering up our roads and behaving as though he owned them. Simon should know better than to encourage them, and so you can tell him."

"Can't *you* tell him?"

"I aren't welcome at Grebe anymore, not since Simon turned me out of those fields. Fifty years come Michaelmas it'll be that I've grazed that twelve acres and the cliff strip. Doris Wherry wouldn't stand for it. Foreigners!"

By virtue of her marriage to Doris Wherry's grandson, Anna was rarely regarded as a foreigner, but was still on the defensive when outsiders were so described. But she was spared answering, as the gallery door opened and some of the guests came out. Mr. Hosking lowered himself down the open treads of the spiral staircase and eased himself into his car. He drove away looking like Mr. Toad.

Anna went back into the gallery. Ivory Judd, standing beside her idealisation of herself, was stripping off her clothes to show an enthusiastic young woman the original

from which she painted. She stood holding her purple caf-
tan, displaying dun-coloured flesh unadorned except by
plaited-leather necklaces, the flesh less taut and muscles
less prominent than she had painted them, but still reality
beside image, as her voice was now loudly proclaiming.

The butcher, baker and candlestick-maker did not like it.
Mrs. Lumb squared her shoulders and put her arm firmly
through her husband's to draw him out of the room away
from corruption, or temptation. They were followed by the
reporter from the local paper, who said, "They won't take
another streaker. It's stale," as he passed Anna.

One of Anna's regular customers was Tamsin Oriel's father, Sir Arnold Lurie. He stared at Ivory's display for several minutes, his eyes flickering from the living to the
painted form. His civil servant's face expressed nothing
more than interest; indeed, to the detached mind, the sight
of Ivory's used and useful body was neither exciting nor
disgusting.

"Anna, my dear," he said at last, "I like the picture of
you better. At least—is it you? It has a look of someone else
that I cannot quite recall."

"It's a very old one of me, Sir Arnold, done years ago
when I was a student. I'm fatter now."

"Well, it's charming. And, as you know, I like to have examples of the work of local painters. The picture of you,
my dear, is delightful. Judd's earlier phase. I wish I could
think who else it is that I'm reminded of. Anyway, Anna,
stick your little tag on it."

"Oh, that's great, really." Anna hurried to fetch her box
of "sold" stickers. She was glad not to have marked it already, mendaciously; she found that it helped sales to make
it appear that one or two pictures had been snapped up at
once. Sir Arnold Lurie followed to her desk, and pulled his
cheque-book from the inside pocket of his tweed jacket.

"How do you think Tamsin's getting on?" he asked. He
had found the cottage at the end of the Buxtons' drive for
his daughter, but tried not to bother her unless she asked
him or his wife to help with the children. He wanted her to

feel she was completely independent, not under her parents' eyes.

"It isn't easy, you know, for a mother on her own," Anna said.

"I know. We can't help worrying about her. I've heard, from common friends, that Alexander Oriel is likely to be sent to the States. And, of course, his Clarissa is an American."

"So the separation will be permanent."

"I am beginning to fear so. My wife and I are naturally not happy about it. How do you think Tamsin will react, Anna? You are so much closer to her in age."

"I don't know her well enough to be sure," Anna said slowly. "After all, she's only lived here for three months. I must say, she was absolutely sweet to me when I was having Emmy—helping with Billy and so on. But we . . . we start with different assumptions. Our experience of life has been so different."

"I am afraid that we made things too easy for our daughter. Perhaps it's a mistake to do that. However, I know that the only rule is that the parent is always wrong."

"Sir Arnold," Anna said, putting her hand on his sleeve, "if you knew what a difference it would once have made to me to have the kind of support you are giving Tamsin now . . . The parent is quite right to help, if he is within reach. I assure you of that." Embarrassed by her own earnestness, she turned away to look for Billy, and lifted him up to stick the round red label onto the portrait of her younger self. Ivory Judd shouted, "A sale! Marvellous! I must embrace you." She pulled her loose dress on over her head and made her way toward Sir Arnold.

"I like the subject, Miss Judd," he said.

"Ah, the subject is woman, eternal, mysterious, full of unrealised urges and ambitions, little Anna, long ago, before—"

"Ivory," Anna said sharply. "The man from the *Guardian* is leaving. Can you say a word or two before he goes?"

The party was about to end in a rush, with most of the guests mentioning their dinner or their baby-sitters. As always, a core of enthusiasts stayed on in the gallery; Ivory herself; Phelim Connor, who called himself a writer but had never published anything except at his own expense, and who was complaining bitterly because an official, who had called on him to verify a detail of his supplementary benefit claim, had informed the police that he was growing cannabis on his porch. He now faced the problem of finding the money for a stiff fine as well as being without a smoke for the next few months. He was dropping hints that there should be a whip-round to cover his expenses. Harry Prout was squatting on the haircord carpet picking up spilt peanuts. His hair swung forward to the floor, and as Anna stepped past him she conquered the urge to kick his pointed buttocks rather sharply. His work—obsessively detailed miniature woodcuts—was competent, but she refused to exhibit it. A man who devoted his talent to the classification of, and search for, the perfect turd was not her kind of artist.

Anna decided to leave them to it. She went down the stairs and across the yard to her house. Billy was so tired that she simply lifted him onto the sofa, and he fell asleep with his thumb in his mouth. There was no sound from Emmy upstairs. Anna sat down at the kitchen table and drank some red wine from a bottle which she found half full on the table. James would have said that it was half empty, she thought—pinning down, as she often did in various ways, the difference between them.

Anna was quite glad to escape the dreadful stage of her parties when realism crept in, and she knew that the profit from the few sales would not cover the cost of the drink she had handed out; and that the painters who consented or begged to show their work in her gallery were never going to have examples of it bought for the Tate. She drank some more of the wine and watched her reflection in the window. The fluorescent light, always necessary in this dark room, cast every shadow on her face into relief, and hardened the planes and angles which added up, in a kinder light, to something pleasant if unremarkable. She was not beautiful, but unlikely ever to be ugly, she

thought, with the firm, full flesh of a Mrs. Noah, and the
flush of a happy woman who lived much outdoors in the
soft Cornish air.

Emmy whimpered, and Anna went to fetch her from upstairs. She changed the nappy, and pushed the cat out of
the kitchen armchair so as to sit and feed the baby. Emmy's
gasps subsided into snorts, and then into the concentrated
silence of passionate sucking. Anna never forgot that James
had likened a baby's hunger to sexual lust. He loved to see
a baby's head pressed against the full white breast. He
sensed parallels between it and a wider life-force. He
would not mind if his wife grew as fat as a mother-goddess.

Anna looked peacefully around the room, without feeling
any guilty compulsion to clear the mess up. James's mother
had come to stay while Anna was having Emmy, and for
too long afterwards. They did not need her; James could
cope perfectly. Even when Anna was well, they believed in
sharing responsibility for all the chores. Mrs. Buxton, although she worked full-time as a librarian, and her husband had a teacher's long holidays, was rigid in her demarcation lines about housework. In their spick bungalow in
Derbyshire, everything had a place, and was kept in it by
Mrs. Buxton's firm hand. James said that she was reacting
against the farmhouse disorder in which she had been
brought up. Grebe had been an efficient unit, but not run
on modern lines. There were no main services—even now,
Simon used well water, though he had installed electricity—
and the cows had been milked by hand. There used to be
jars of ginger beer bubbling gently in one corner, bowls of
other produce on the tables, a hand-fed lamb in a box by
the range, all necessary and sensible but far from tidy.
Only the dairy had been clean and orderly, because if the
utensils were not properly scalded the butter would not
come. Granny used to say, "You can't fool butter."

It caused James's mother real pain to see the disorder of
River House. She would look around James and Anna's
kitchen making small dismayed exclamations. She knew her
duty as a mother-in-law, and addressed her remarks to
James.

"Oh, darling, the mess. Look, mouldy jam. How could you?"

"It's only penicillin, Mother."

"And what's this? Oh dear, brown rice? It's quite unnecessary. Look at you. Never a day's illness as a child and no nonsense about compost and grinding flour on stone. I'm sure you have rats on your compost heap. I'll go into Withiel tomorrow and get some nice fresh frozen vegetables."

James and Anna would hold hands under the table and let it all pass over them. They would smuggle vitamin-packed whole foods into Mrs. Buxton's diet. She claimed only to like the taste of convenience foods.

"There," James would say triumphantly. "You liked that egg, didn't you? I see you have eaten it all. Straight from the henhouse. And the fruit? Picked ten minutes ago and sweetened with honey. I had one hundred jars of it last year from my hives."

"I eat it out of politeness, naturally, darling. But, really, I couldn't tell the difference between these potatoes and tinned ones. It all seems very silly to me, especially when you let your potatoes be eaten by mice. Was it last year that they got the lot? Your own butter? I thought it was marge."

But James would carry on his missionary boasting. And when his mother left he opened her packed suitcase and put three jars of his best honey between her petticoats.

Anna buttoned her shirt, and hoisted Emmy under one arm so as to go and fetch some vegetables from the larder for supper. James came into the kitchen and took Emmy into his arms. He nuzzled his face into her soft neck.

"Darling," Anna said, "is anything wrong?"

James lifted his head, and she saw the face of despair.

"He's warned me off," he said. "Simon. He's told me to keep off Grebe. He said I was trespassing. He's turned me away."

CHAPTER 3

Philippa Oriel prodded with her fork at a heap of vegetables in cheese sauce. "You wouldn't have fed us on this if Daddy was here," she said. "Honestly, Mum, it's yucky."

Tamsin looked at Ben. He was chewing with perseverance, but did not meet her eye. Tamsin took a mouthful herself.

"It's very good for you, Pippa," she said firmly.

"So was steak, at home, and chicken and shrimps and things."

"Yes, well, you can't have all those luxuries when—" She broke off and took a deep breath. Both the children were watching her, waiting for the admission she had not made to them yet.

"I bet Daddy is having roast goose for supper," Ben said. He looked cautiously at a piece of celery. "I've had enough, Mum. Unless there is some pudding?" he added.

"Fruit. Help yourself."

Alex would probably be ordering himself and Clarissa gulls' eggs and Scotch salmon. Just now they would be drinking champagne cocktails in a dim bar where Alex would sign the bill. Tamsin could see, as precisely as if they were in the same room, Clarissa's red hair, swinging backwards and forwards as she leant animatedly to and from Alex, bouncing the pendant he had given her into the cleft between her breasts. Or perhaps they were in bed; in Tamsin's bed.

"Can we watch telly?" Pippa asked. She came round the table and leant against her mother. Tamsin knew that she only complained about the food because she was too sensitive to complain about being without her father.

The children went to sit in front of some gyrating musicians; Tamsin went out into the garden to fetch in the rugs and chairs. The weather in Cornwall was proving to be idyllic, and the drawers full of clothes for wet and cold weather which Lady Lurie had advised her to bring were unopened. Tamsin spent a large part of every day lying in the sun.

The conditions were precisely those which should have been ideal for getting on with the novel. Every day Tamsin set out a small card table, her typewriter and the basket containing a stack of blank paper and a small sheaf of notes and false starts. The stone with which they were weighted down against the wind stayed in place all day.

When Pippa and Ben were tiny, they were jealous of her typewriter and tried to "help." She would sit at the kitchen table, hammering down the phrases before they went out of her mind, waist-high in dirty dishes and broken toys, neck-high in social obligations for coffee mornings, tea parties, wine and cheese evenings, and dinners to give and go to for the sake of Alex's career. What books she would write when she was free, she would say. What subtleties of expression and intricacies of thought would flow from her fingertips once she was able to set down more than one paragraph at a time.

Yet since coming to Cornwall, Tamsin had written nothing. She was alone all day while the children were at school, and undisturbed except for an occasional call from Anna. Her parents were careful not to intrude. The view was beautiful, the silence hardly broken.

She went into the cottage and took her third, most recent novel from the shelf. The jacket copy described it as "a sensitive and witty dissection of the feminine predicament." The reviewers had praised her prose and recommended her insights. Alexander, when asked by his boss what Tamsin's new book was about, replied, "Oh, it's the graduate wife weeping into the kitchen sink again."

"But I don't write autobiography," Tamsin added hastily. She had never been part of the movement for women's liberation. Like conservation of the environment and vegetarianism, it had always seemed a worthy cause of which she had no personal need.

The review in *The Times Literary Supplement* (four unsigned lines filling in the bottom of a column) said that Tamsin was writing about the conflicts of modern women. She would never have put it that way herself. She would have liked simply to be accepted as an interpreter of modern life.

She flicked through the pages. She often looked at her own works, to remind herself that what she had done three times she would be able to do again. She thought: I suppose they are really about myself. No wonder Alex found me irritating.

Tamsin was indeed dripping tears into the kitchen sink—though they were the tears not so much of a graduate, as of a separated, wife—when Anna came in to ask whether she would like some spinach. Tamsin flipped the lid down on to the wastebucket. Anna had given her most of the vegetables which the children had spurned at supper.

"Oh, have you managed to start again?" Anna said, looking at the typewriter.

"No, I despair," Tamsin replied. "The trouble is, I don't think I believe in it anymore."

"What, writing novels? Surely . . ."

"No, I mean the sort of writing I've done so far. Delving into the subconscious. I always thought that the only way to make a good book was to recognise everything in oneself, break down the barriers of one's own inhibitions and suppressions. To be truthful from childhood on. But I don't know. Look at Pippa and Ben. They don't seem deeply affected by anything. They miss Alex up to a point, but not traumatically; they are quite happy. Not that I want to imagine scars on their psyches. But how can my probing and delving into my characters, and through them into myself, really matter?"

Tamsin had never doubted the point of exploring the human condition before. She had written books which were sensitive, perceptive and detailed; she stuck to the principle that no character should appear in fiction unless his in-

ventor could account for every moment of his past. Her
themes were domestic, but she believed they had a wider
significance. She was frank about contraception, frigidity,
menstruation and defecation, witty about the tyranny of
trivial events, clearsighted about the agonies of childhood
and unflinching about hypocrisy. She was beginning to feel
that all her works had been a type of historical novel,
reports from past battlefields, episodes in the well-
documented wars between enslaved wives and free husbands.

"There is no need to remember happy childhood," Anna
said. "All they will need is the memory that it happened.
Like yours."

"Nice parents, happy day-school, ponies on the common
on Saturday afternoons, and tea and toast by the fire.
You're probably quite right. What about yours?"

"Oh," Anna said, "mine was extremely different. Not like
this at all." She glanced around the room as though amused
by the comparison. "But this is what my children are going
to have."

Tamsin had been gently warned off asking about Anna's
background before. In the past she would have carried on
probing, but since getting her freelance job with Radio
Withiel she tried to restrain her curiosity unless she was
holding a microphone. She did not want the asking of im-
pertinent questions to become a habit.

Sir Arnold Lurie had put the job in Tamsin's way, after
she had moved to the cottage. He thought it was bad for
his daughter to be alone all day. She ought to get out and
meet people. He was afraid she would brood about Alex
and Clarissa. He had come across the producer of the local
radio's "chat programme" at a function in aid of the
lifeboat, and happened to discover that there would be
room for a part-time freelance interviewer. All Tamsin
needed to do, her father said, was sit in this young man's
office and tell him that she was God's gift to him. Self-
confidence, he insisted, was all she needed.

Tamsin was not so brash, but when she met Tony Rawe
they recognised one another from parent–teacher associa-

tion meetings. Before he had come out in his true colours, he told Tamsin he'd been hetero-, or bi-, really, he said, and fathered a marvellously dishy daughter called Melissa. Melissa carried a miniature radio in her satchel, so as to hear her father's voice every day. Tamsin told Tony Rawe as little as she could about Alex and her own children, and a little more about her education at Oxford and her published work. They got on rather well together.

The little radio station was desperately unprofessional, for it was run on a minute budget and the potential audience was numbered in no more than four figures. But it gave Tamsin a start in a job she had never thought of having, and she liked having deadlines, and disciplines, to which few novelists were normally subjected. She was well aware that, if she did not force herself to write another book, nobody else would demand it.

It was fun to provide unmemorable wallpaper for the mind. Tamsin had the use of a portable tape-recording machine, and was supposed to do interviews which lasted no more than three minutes, which were snappy but not controversial, and of general but specifically local interest. Talking parrots were preferred to exposures of political scandals or anything else so topical.

"Don't kid yourself that you're getting a training for the Beeb," Tony Rawe told her gloomily. "We're all amateurs here."

"Why do you do it?" Tamsin asked him, and a fanatic gleam lit his eye.

"I am a pioneer for Radio Kernow—that's Cornwall in Cornish. When we get our national station I'll be in on the ground floor. Anyway, I need to live near the surf."

So Tamsin had interviewed him about the fascination of the big rollers, and the addicted surfer's life, and the next week he had allowed her to chair five whole minutes of discussion about the future of the Cornish language. It was all great fun, just like the days when Tamsin was the editor of a breakaway undergraduate newspaper.

The children were stonily unconcerned about Tamsin's new work, and usually left the room when her voice came on the air. Tamsin herself thought that, having spent her twenties as a writer, she might pass her thirties as a journalist. She would start putting out feelers; try to make contact with friends from Oxford who had gone into the communications industry. Investigative journalism would be fun, she thought; to have a dig at the soft underbelly of national life; or perhaps try to get her own opinion column, or a regular review spot. On good days there seemed no end to the possibilities. On bad ones, when she remembered that journalism was the most competitive of professions, she knew that she would never be more than the ex-wife of a well-known oil executive, who used to masturbate her soul by writing self-indulgent novels.

"Do you know about Simon?" Anna asked.

Tamsin jerked her self-pitying thoughts back to the outside world. Was Anna asking about Simon because she knew . . . ? There would come a point, Tamsin thought, when the wounds to her pride, to the ability to believe that a man could want her and carry on wanting her, would become mortal. But Anna meant nothing so personal. Indeed, it was unlikely that she knew that there ever had been a connection between Simon Wherry and Tamsin.

"James said you went with him to Grebe yesterday. He's in a dreadful state. What did Simon really say?"

"He asked him not to go there. Said to leave him in peace."

"Did he say why? I can't get any sense out of James."

"Not that I could hear. But they have never been the best of friends, have they?"

"No, that's true, but they have always kept a working relationship going. After all they practically grew up together when they were here in the holidays. They had their quarrels, masses of them, but always managed to make them up. But it seems different this time. I've never seen James like this. I don't suppose you understand how much it means to him, going to Grebe. He'll never get over Granny's leaving it to Simon, though he might have expected it. After all, Simon's father was her only son. But James somehow thought she would realise how much better he would care for the place. I'll never forgive Simon for making James so unhappy. I won't let him get away with it."

"Will you be able to stop him?"

Tamsin thought of Simon's egocentric and intractable personality, hidden under layers of worldliness and good manners. I'm a fine picker, she thought sardonically. From Simon, who wanted a two-night stand; through Alex, who didn't even try to resist the demands of a new physical passion, and willingly chucked her and the children for its sake; back to Tamsin's first lover, an Oxford don who said that sex would make her write more understanding essays about English love poetry. Only three, but all failures. "Who needs men?" Tamsin said aloud.

One needed a man to make an Emmy. The two women stood looking down into her pram. She was enough to make any mother broody, with her miniature features, pink cheeks and tuffet of blonde hair on top of her head.

"How different she is from Billy," Tamsin said.

"Yes, isn't she? Billy was always a long, thin creature with black curls. This girl's like me. Perhaps the next will be carroty, like Dad."

"Haven't you stopped? Two point three children per family . . . Though how you have point three of a baby I don't know."

"Stop at my tidy son and daughter, like you? No, James and I are going to have lots. Rows of children."

Tamsin offered to walk up the drive with Anna; it was pleasant in the low evening sunshine. They walked between the scented trees, fanning midges away from their faces with languid hands. Tamsin wondered whether she could make Anna plausible in a book, stereotyped as she seemed, adhering to the straight good-taste ticket of a woman making her conscientious stand against a consumer society.

They went to the house together, and Tamsin turned back alone to the cottage. Halfway down the drive she was diverted by a loud tinny banging. She peered through the hedge and then climbed over the gate to see what James was doing. He was standing on a chair, holding a deep oval basket in his outstretched hands under the horizontal branch of a tree. About twenty yards away from him, Billy, draped in some sort of veiling, was banging a dustbin lid with a stick, and at the same time jumping up and down and shouting. As Tamsin watched, a black conical lump which was hanging from the branch fell into the basket below it. James waited for a moment, and then shouted. "Okay, mate, that's enough. Good boy." He stepped to the ground cradling the wickerwork skep, and took the veil from Billy's head to spread over the top of the open container.

A few bees were still flying round, but James ignored them and unwrapped the netting from the little boy. "Run along back to Mummy now. Here, take the noisemaker with you. Go and tell Mummy how you made the banging for me."

"What are you doing?" Tamsin said.

"Collecting a swarm of bees. Wonderful creatures. Do you know about them?"

"Only that they make honey and sting."

"Sting? Oh, that's nothing. Beekeepers get immune. Anyway, they only sting if they are frightened or if you provoke them. They don't like smells like alcohol or hair lacquer. But did you know that they communicate with one another, that they have a language? They dance in patterns which the other bees understand, to tell them where to look for food. Shall I show you inside a hive?"

"Another time, perhaps, thank you."

"Not now? All right. It's worth seeing, though—rows of perfect wax hexagons."

"I didn't know you could see inside hives."

"Only the modern ones, with hinged sections. You couldn't in the past, when they were the traditional shape— like this skep, really. In the wild, bees nest in crannies— hollow trees, roof eaves and so on. I really love the little creatures."

"Well, James, I'm sorry but they still frighten me." Tamsin edged away from the informative flow of James's conversation.

"Are you off? I must tell you in greater detail another time. Perhaps you'd like to do a piece for your radio programme."

Tamsin looked back along the drive as she shut her front door; funny old James, plodding along in the dusk with his skep full of bees. She must remember to ask Tony Rawe whether that subject would strike the right note.

Pippa and Ben were separated from the television and persuaded to go to bed. Tamsin wrote down some desultory thoughts: ideas for interviews, questions she must remember to ask in interviews she had arranged to do later in the week, hints at ideas for fiction. She wrote down some good names for heroines. She could never think constructively about a character until she had chosen a suitable and in some way descriptive name. Anna had a very neutral name, so no wonder she was difficult to slot into a novelist's definition.

Tamsin drew back the curtains before going to bed. It was high water, and the river was lit by a new moon and edged by the dark shadow of Grebe's oak woods. Simon must have been having one of his frequent parties aboard; a small boat was moving away from the *Cock's Comb*. The man who was rowing placed his oars delicately in and out of the still water until he reached the shallows. He sprang out and disappeared from view. Nothing else could be seen to stir.

She dreamt about recording the buzz of bees from inside the hive and awoke to acute relief that her actual interviews demanded less courage. Councillor Mrs. Lumb was more Tamsin's level. She had spent the previous afternoon with Councillor Mrs. Lumb and would have to pass the morning listening to that grating, harsh voice as she trimmed the interview to a usable length. She drove the children to school and went straight on to the studio.

Radio Withiel consisted of three rooms on one floor of the curate's house. Sometimes the technicians had to be sent upstairs to ask the curate if his visitors could keep quiet during a broadcast; but the rooms had been pretty well soundproofed, and were lined and double-glazed, so that entering them felt a little like going into a padded cell. Nobody was there so early in the day; breakfast-time programmes were left to the BBC, and the technicians would come in later to perform their incomprehensible rituals with buttons and switches. Meanwhile Tamsin had the editing machine to herself.

She played the interview over. Out of thirty minutes she would have to extract three. Mrs. Lumb, far from needing to be prompted, would not stop talking—at first about the ostensible subject of the interview, which was religious education in schools; after that she dilated on the need for old-fashioned values and the importance of instilling respect in the young; then she moved smoothly on to the reasons for the national decline, and a general denunciation of immigrants, teachers, sociologists, students and what she called "young layabouts." She predicted bloodbaths in the big cities with evident pleasure.

Tamsin made a firm cut with the razor blade to excise Mrs. Lumb's views on the Arts Council and its dispensation of taxpayers' money. She also took some pleasure in cutting out a diatribe about holidaymakers ("living it up on their social security payments") and how much Mrs. Lumb would like to pull up drawbridges around a right, tight little Withiel to keep it uncontaminated.

Goaded into behaviour which she had been taught was unprofessional, Tamsin had volunteered the information that the dreaded campers had even penetrated to the Grebe.

"No! Are you quite sure?" Mrs. Lumb exclaimed. "That's been designated under Article Four, not to mention being part of the Heritage Coastline and an area of outstanding natural beauty. Thank you for telling me, my dear. That is something I can nip in the bud. There are a few advantages to being in my position, I'm glad to say, and a hot line to the Planning and Public Health departments is one of them. I'll get the Environmental Health Officer out there straightaway. In fact, I'll go and have a look for myself. I haven't seen Simon Wherry since he was a child. A very spoilt and impudent little boy he was too."

Tamsin untangled herself from loops of magnetic tape. As usual, she was getting into a mess with the tape and the sticky material she used for joining the cut edges. She had made several mistakes in cutting, taking off too much of Mrs. Lumb's sentences. However, eventually she managed to cobble together a piece which would do, she hoped, to make Mrs. Lumb the target of every voter's loathing, and threw yards of wasted tape into the bin. She left the labelled box on Tony Rawe's desk, and let herself out into the sunshine to stand for a moment blinking on the doorstep.

"Tamsin!" She heard her name, more hissed than called, and looked around. "Tamsin." She recognised nobody in the street, but when her name was called for the third time she saw Anna, peering from behind the hedge in the next garden.

"Hullo—" she began, but Anna put her finger on her lips and then beckoned. "I'm hiding from someone I don't want to get caught by."

"What if somebody comes out of the house?"

"That's the trouble. Is your car nearby?"

Tamsin walked quickly to the car-park, wondering what Anna was up to. She seemed more worried than the fear of a social encounter could warrant.

Tamsin pulled her Mini into the kerb, and saw Anna give a rabbitlike glance up and down the street before scuttling across and into the car. She kept her face well down.

"So awkward," she said.

"What's the matter, Anna?" Tamsin said.

"A face from the past," Anna muttered. "It gave me such a shock. If he'd seen me, and Billy— Oh, Tamsin, thank God you were there."

Tamsin glanced thoughtfully at her and did not answer. Anna's hands were trembling and her face was pale. Most of the time Tamsin felt that she knew Anna well; they had become instant friends. But sometimes she was reminded that they had only met for the first time a few months before, when Tamsin came down to stay with her parents and look the cottage over. That was not enough time in which to learn what would send a woman into terrified hiding in the main street of her hometown.

CHAPTER 4

The exhibition of Ivory Judd's paintings ran, not very successfully, for a month. Three portraits and five landscapes had been sold, and Ivory was to come over to collect the remaining fifty-one canvases. An Arts Council touring exhibition had arrived in elegant, highly insured transport, but the professionals who brought it neither wanted nor gave help with the hanging and taking down of pictures. Anna stood with Emmy on her hip and checked the chairs James was to deliver to a firm in Withiel, which had commissioned them from James to smarten up its conference room. They claimed tax relief on his commission, and advertised that they supported local craftsmen.

"I shall go to Grebe on the way back from Withiel," James said. "It's been more than four weeks. I must know what's going on."

Anna knew that James and Simon always made up their quarrels, grudgingly, in the end. She said, "Can you pick Billy up from the playgroup on the way back? I have a headache."

"Another? You really will have to see the doctor. Or that naturopath Ivory suggested. You can't go on like this. Go and lie down. These guys can manage. In fact, they would obviously rather be left to it. Ghastly, these sculptures, aren't they?"

"Yes, but we need the grant for showing them. Otherwise we couldn't afford to show Laurie's woodcuts in the back room."

"You do look under the weather again," James said. "Go on in. I'll pick Billy up in the lorry after I've been to Grebe."

"James, do you think you should go there? I mean, after what Simon said . . ."

"I must go and see what's happening. Damn it all, it will soon be— Never mind. Look, darling, trespass isn't a criminal offence. The worst that can happen is that I'm asked to leave again." He kissed her on the cheek and rubbed his nose against Emmy's. Anna went into the house, looking, James suddenly realised, really unwell, and he wondered whether he should stay with her after all. But Emmy would sleep and he would be back by lunchtime. He could not wait any longer to get to Grebe.

The potholes in the old drive would have ruined his lorry, but James still resented the smooth new tarmac and the overhead wires above it which brought electricity to the house. He tried to banish from his mind the picture, in medievally brilliant colour and detail, of the strip-fields, beehives and thriving crops which he had once planned for these acres. When they were boys, Simon would furnish this land with imaginary racetracks and stock cars. He would suggest hiring out a field to a circus, playing with the fancy of camels and elephants grazing at Grebe. Later he proposed offering accommodation to a pop festival; that was still being discussed with the kind of smooth, rich entrepreneur most distrusted by James. As an undergraduate Simon was keen on the theatre, starting in an intellectual way with much discussion of Stanislavsky and the Method, and the inner meaning of nudity, and the cleansing of catharsis. By the time he was in his last year at Cambridge he had fallen in with a less esoteric troupe, and acted Malvolio in a clifftop theatre in west Cornwall and Shylock in a performance designed for school classrooms. He talked about bringing the drama back to the people, the immediacy of miracle plays, and of becoming a strolling player ready to pitch his stage on any beach or car-park and attract audiences by his force and fervour. Once he lived in London, Simon became less democratic. He received advance notices from Covent Garden, and attended first nights in fashionable theatres. He took his girlfriends to

plays which experimented more with the limits of censor-
ship than of imagination.

Simon and his father were big spenders. It would not
have been surprising if James had hankered for high living too, especially since Mrs. Buxton disapproved of her
brother John Wherry and his son Simon. John Wherry had
made, she thought, the wrong friends during the war and
acquired a taste for luxury inappropriate in one whose father had been a plain working farmer. John should never
have got himself a job in the City. His duty had been to go
home, drive tractors, milk cows, go to market, and take
over from Grandfather Wherry when he became infirm. He
was spoiling himself, Barbara Buxton said, and would spoil
that boy of his. Every particular of Simon's later career
confirmed his aunt Barbara in her disapproval.

"If only I had been the son," she would say. "If only I
could have stayed on the land."

James's father would sigh. It was hardly his fault that
Barbara had chosen to become a trainee at Withiel Library
when she left school; hardly his fault, when she had fallen
in love with him, after they had met during his summer
holiday, that she had to live in his home, not hers, once
they were married. He had nothing with which to reproach
himself, yet his conversation was spiced with self-blame.

Barbara Buxton blamed James too, when he did not want
to go to a university and "get on" in life. In spite of all the
criticisms she made of her brother John's way of life, she
would have liked to show him that her son James could
compete in his sphere and win. James was at a technical
college while Simon was at Cambridge. James had been
forced to start his apprenticeship late, because his mother
would not admit that he was unsuited for an academic education until he failed all the qualifying examinations. James
wanted to be a craftsman, and his ambition would have
been precisely fulfilled if only his mother had not been so
scornful; if only Simon had been, not patronising, which
would have been bearable, but less carefully kind. Simon
would ask about the course and admire James for being

such a practical chap, and deprecate his own clumsy hands. "I have ten thumbs," he would say.

James wondered whether his mother and uncle had been as happy with their tiny children as he and Anna were with their two. He found it poignant to suppose that Barbara Buxton and John Wherry might have made happy plans together for their children's future.

James parked the lorry on the gravel clearing near the house. Nobody came out, and James swung himself to the ground and stood looking around.

The paint had not been renewed since Simon had taken possession. James poked with his penknife at the wood of one of the window frames, and it sank dangerously in. Three slates were off the roof, revealing the wood battens. There was nothing under them but a smear of lime and mud. The next southwesterly gale could whip the whole roof off. Two windowpanes were broken and the wooden porch was badly warped. "People shouldn't have houses," James muttered, "if they can't take care of them." He banged on the door, chipping some of the paint off with his knuckles, but there was no reply. He wandered round the outside of the house, listing the deteriorations which he could see even since his last visit.

The degradation of the estate looked worse in the sunshine. There had been no rain for several weeks, and the ground was beginning to crack where there were usually mud puddles. What a productive, prosperous show Grebe could have made in this enchanted weather. Never had there been such a year for trees; any garden which had received the minimum of attention was bursting with flowers and the promise of fruit. What crops could have been raised at Grebe this year, what fields of corn, what bulging cows. James thought of the honey-coloured Jerseys he had planned to keep, how they would have swayed into this yard at milking time. He would have milked by hand, and kept a bull with a ring in his nose. The children would have taught the calves to lap milk from a bucket, and Anna would have made great muslin-swathed cheeses to last them through the winter.

He went through the gateway into the triangular field. The gate was broken and lying on the ground, with brambles growing through the bars. This was where he had planned to keep his goat. And he would have had a chicken run, and geese in the orchard. He would have dug out the pond and kept ducks. He had planned to take in the small field beside Granny's vegetable patch, to experiment with foods which were not part of the local farming pattern—sweet corn, artichokes, squashes and vines. Anna had decided to dry out their own sea salt. James looked greedily at the wasted land, reviving the plans he had been obliged to suppress.

The campsite was still more sordid than it had been a month before. James lifted the flap of one of the tents and withdrew quickly from the smell of unwashed clothes and unfinished meals.

"Hullo?" he shouted. "Anyone here?" But nobody came out of the closed tents or vans.

James went back to the house and pushed open the window into the scullery which he had often climbed through as a boy. He had grown, and the window was small, but he managed to get into the house. The scullery, a lean-to structure behind the kitchen, was not in use anymore. On the slate shelves were old bottles of Granny's preserves. She always had a siege mentality, which was intensified in the last years of her life, and she was never happy unless the house was stocked with bottled fruit, salted vegetables, jams, chutneys and sardines. The tinned food was all gone, but there were still full jars of preserves, clouded on the outside and with dust and tarnish on their lids and, just visible through the glass, thick mould on the surface of the food. The old cat basket was on the floor, surrounded by feathers which had fallen from the holes in the knitted cushion cover. On the top shelf were three gas-mask boxes, unopened since the day they came into the house. Several cane trugs hung on hooks under a broken shopping basket and an oilskin cape. The little room was so redolent of Granny that James was almost surprised, when he stepped into the kitchen, not to find her there, bending over the big porcelain sink, or rolling out pastry with positive movements of her strong, wrinkled, brown arms.

The elaborate designs on the Cornish range were now obscured by the dust on its black cast-iron surface. Granny kept the brass knobs polished and the iron coated with blacking, and boasted that she had not allowed the fire to go out since her wedding day. She swore it cooked much better pasties and saffron cakes than any modern cooker.

Simon used the tarnished knobs to hang coats on, and kept spare shoes in the ovens. He had installed a small bottled-gas stove, which was coated with grease and smelt of old fish. James had taken the old table, white with years of scrubbing, away to River House with the other portable property, but the huge dresser was probably keeping the house walls up and had been left in position.

There were two unopened letters on the dresser, each with the emblem of Withiel District Council on the back, and a postcard from one of Simon's girlfriends; sand, sea, sun and lines of apartment blocks: "Having a wonderful time. Wish you were here."

James had only liked one of the many girls to whom Simon had introduced him. Most of Simon's female friends were smooth, expensive, superficial creatures, like Simon's sister who had gone to live in America; all equally pleasure-seeking, extravagant and vapid. He disliked the paint they wore on their faces and the jewellery they dangled from neck and wrist. He was not attracted by their firm, round bodies, whether outlined in tight denim or revealed in near-nudity on the beach. James liked women whom Simon despised, full of sympathy and simplicity.

How strange, then, that it should have been Simon who brought Anna and James together, on a day very like this one, sunny, green and sweet-smelling.

It was the last week of the holidays. James had come down to Grebe to make arrangements for the disposal of the furniture which Granny had left him, and had been staying in Penwith with Ivory Judd. Simon might have given him a bed at Grebe, but he could hardly bear to enter the place, with the raw, new wound of knowing it was not to be his own. Ivory gingered him up, with encouragement and teasing, and he borrowed her car to drive himself over. He was due to catch the night train so as to be on parade in the classroom the next day.

Granny kept the place in good order even in the last few months when she had been ill. She refused all offers of beds in hospitals, or rooms in homes for the elderly, and said that she would only leave Grebe in her box. She pointed out the coffin hatch in her bedroom to the welfare visitors and assured them that she had money put aside to cover her funeral expenses. If she chose to die on her own, in her own house, who was going to stop her? They might have stopped her, at that; Mr. Hosking told James at the graveside that there was talk of getting court orders and forcing the ministrations of a nanny state on to old Doris Wherry, but she dropped dead in her own orchard one day, where she had tottered to evict some trespassers, busy tormenting her donkeys, who existed only in her imagination. During the time she had been infirm, Leonard Hosking sent his own workmen to help out. She was a game old thing, he said, and had been at Grebe as long as he could remember; he would make sure it was not his fault if she had to leave it alive.

So the paint had still been white, that spring day, and the cobblestones a clear, weedless black; the cats still slept on the barn doorsill, and the daffodils were in flower under the pink rhododendrons in the drive.

The robust yell of a small baby came through the open window, though James was so preoccupied that he did not stop to wonder why. When he looked in through the open door, he saw Anna in the kitchen; a sturdy, yellow-haired girl, with tanned, thick cheekbones like a Slavic peasant, and generous bosom and hips. She smiled at him and called, "Simon, you've got a visitor." And Simon came down the stairs, covered with dust from the space under the rafters because, he said, he had been hunting for the old wooden cradle which should be somewhere around, and said, "Anna, James. James, Anna."

Oddly enough, though he had read about it often and ac-

cepted its value as dogma, James had never seen a woman
breast-feeding a baby. Anna was perfectly unselfconscious,
and sat in Granny's chair to unbutton her clothes and expose her breast, while the baby lay across her knees. James
stared at the blue veins in the white skin, and at the large
brown areola, and the hard nipple with drops of thin milk
falling from it. He felt an extraordinary urge to put his lips
to it and, when the baby did so, experienced a more familiar desire for the fecund woman.

Simon glanced at him with amusement. He had notice-
ably averted his own eyes when Anna undid her shirt, and
now he murmured something about looking for the cradle
in the barn and left the room.

"Have you been here long?" James asked, stammering a
little, and Anna gave him her closed-lip smile and shook
her head. She told him that she was going to look for somewhere to live near Withiel because she liked it so much.
Simon was just putting her up for a little while. Perhaps
James knew of a suitable property?

How long did it take him to decide that to go back to the
Midlands, and teach bored kids to carve wood without cutting their arteries, would kill him as surely as if he had
severed his own? Certainly he postponed his departure, but
he could hardly now remember whether he had believed
his ostensible reason, of having an attack of food poisoning.
He had moved into Grebe because Simon was leaving on
that night's tide, and for a few days he and Anna lived his
dream life. He looked after the remaining animals, stacked
up wood in the shed for next winter and trimmed the edges
of the lawn. Anna planted Granny's geranium cuttings in
the granite trough which had once been a cider press, and
washed all the curtains. They talked about the farm, and
identified Granny's flowers, and admired the colour of the
sea. James told Anna that the huge magnolia had been
planted when the species was first introduced from the
Himalayas in the nineteenth century, and that the rowan
tree by the front gate was a traditional guardian against
witches.

Anna fed her baby, who grew before their eyes, and she

sketched him and James, and the flowers, and made a picture of the house from shells stuck onto a driftwood plank.

At the end of the week they decided to get married, and to use Anna's money, which she called her dowry, to buy a house near Grebe. Fate must have smiled on them, because the next day they went into Withiel and found in the local paper the advertisement for the executors' sale of River House, with its three acres of land, disused barn ideal for conversion into a workshop and gallery, and lodge cottage with its sitting tenant. The house needed new wiring, plumbing, roofing and flooring, quite apart from the removal of the dirt of years. Anna and James were doing the conversion themselves, and even now, after nearly two years, only the kitchen came up to the standards required for a council house. James had fitted it with cabinets thrown out by other modernisers. The first task had been to get the gallery ready, and that was successful enough to win design prizes. And James, from his base across the water, could still keep his eye on Grebe.

So it was with possessive fury that he now wondered what on earth was going on here.

Accretions of dust and cobwebs and mouse droppings had built up on all the flat surfaces. A black stripe of ants led to a patch of stickiness under the bottled-gas cooker. James opened the drawers and cupboards of Granny's dresser. It looked almost as though Simon were setting up in business as a clockmaker. There were several alarm clocks, and piles of their components. In one of the drawers was a tangle of wire, and a box full of nuts and bolts. In another was a stack of those padded envelopes which are used for sending books through the post. On the floor lay a collection of plastic shopping bags printed with the names of various large London stores.

James shrugged his shoulders impatiently. This was ridiculous. What did it matter what unconstructive occupation Simon had wasted his time on? All James needed to know, and could see, was that Grebe was degenerating to a point where it would be beyond salvation. The heart of the farmland would stop beating and the old house would collapse. Then Granny would be sorry.

"Who's in there?"

James heard the voice calling, but thought nothing of it at first. Then the cloud of anger and frustration and impatience over his mind cleared, and he went to the door. A woman was standing in the little lobby between the two downstairs rooms. "Hullo," she said.

James went closer to her. She was one of the glossy girls Simon always trailed around with him. She would be called something like Vikki or Nikki or Rikki. She wore jeans, naturally, but the plain denim tubes of fabric, different only in detail from his own, gave the effect of having cost a lot of money, and having been chosen for some imperceptible detail of styling which would have cost enough to feed a family for a week. Her thin body was barely covered by an exiguous vest, and her long, thin hair blew in the gentle breeze onto her face, so that she had to brush it aside with her sharp red nails.

"Who are you?" she said.

"I might ask *you* that."

"My name's Myra."

"What are you doing here?"

"Oh, you aren't very nice." Her voice, slightly Australian, slightly husky, made it clear that this Myra was a more considerable person than she looked at first. It conveyed decisiveness and certainty. "I suppose you're that cousin of Simon's," she said. "The one who is keen on the simple life. Back to the soil and all that."

"I see that you've heard of me."

"What I've heard of you is that Simon told you to get off, didn't he? You've no right here."

He stared at her. "What are *you* doing here?" he asked slowly.

"At this moment," she said, "I'm looking for something. Something Simon's hidden."

"Hidden from you?"

"*For* me."

"Well, ask him where he put it."

"He's not here. I told you."

James looked out from the dark porch to the brilliant garden and yard. "What is it, anyway?" he said.

"Oh, just something of mine . . . something I need. I've searched everywhere. In the bales of straw. Even in the rubbish dump. Do you think he has a special hiding place somewhere? Under some stone or other, perhaps?"

"I wouldn't know. You'd better wait till Simon gets back, hadn't you? Why are you in such a hurry?"

She glanced at him warily, with slightly narrowed eyes, and then gave a wriggle of her hips, as a small child might, and smiled up at him.

"No hurry, not now that you're here," she said, her voice lower, slower, blatantly seductive.

"You aren't just having a holiday, are you?" he said.

"I have been on the beach all day. Look." She pulled her vest over her head with a quick cross-armed movement, and let him see the demarcation line between brown and white skin.

"But why here?" he persisted, shifting his eyes from her small pink-tipped breasts. "Why not the Costa Brava or the south of France?"

"I came here with my friends," she said. She walked out into the sunshine, and then, as though amused by his aversion, stepped out of her trousers and stood there in nothing but her briefs. "Don't you go for girls, then? You gay or something?" James found it easy not to answer taunts which were unfounded. Her slight figure roused him to neither interest nor desire.

"Do you spend your holidays with a butterfly net?" he said.

"Not me, can't be bothered. My friend does sometimes. He gets bored waiting around sunbathing."

"Where is he now? And where is Simon? When did you last see him?"

"Most of them have gone off sailing, and the rest are on the beach," she said. "I'm all on my own. Do you want to keep me company?"

He climbed into the lorry's driving seat and roared the motor so that he would not hear anything else she said. He drove away, leaving her to flaunt her charms alone. He was trying to banish images of death from his mind.

CHAPTER 5

Tamsin was pleased to find herself doing increasingly acceptable work for Radio Withiel. It was a long time since Tony Rawe had rejected one of her tapes, or rather, as he had not the heart to refuse them outright, since he had left Tamsin's contributions in the dusty heap he called his "stockpile." She had even sold to BBC radio an interview with the skipper of a transatlantic racing catamaran, and she was putting together some ideas which she hoped to sell to "Woman's Hour." She was beginning to know her way round the maze of lanes in the Withiel and Brannell region, and to recognise the names which appeared in the local paper. Once, when the wind and tide combined to make the surf irresistible to Tony Rawe, he had telephoned from the north coast and told her to let herself into the studio and present the whole programme.

Tamsin found that, because she was now often too busy for it, she hankered for the sunny cottage garden and the waiting stack of paper. She had not seen Simon Wherry, though after the local paper published a letter from Councillor Mrs. Lumb about unlicensed local campsites, and landowners who were allowed to cock a snook at authority because of their family connections, she had swallowed her pride and gone to Grebe to try to get a reaction from him. Only one person appeared, a tall, red-haired girl with antipodean vowel sounds, who refused to speak into the machine or fetch anyone else who would. She said Simon had buggered off somewhere. Tamsin cobbled some sort of comment together, because Tony did not want to waste a parochial row; she filled in one minute by describing the work of the vandals who had hastened the extinction of the

Large Blue Butterfly, and afterwards felt guilty for using a piece of information she had picked up from James and Anna's unguarded conversation. Fortunately, the Buxtons did not listen to the radio. Other useful interviews had been with a visiting ambassador from a South American country of which Tamsin had never previously heard, and a report about a party held on a visiting Trinity House vessel. Tamsin's father, an old friend of one of the Elder Brethren, had been present, but she was careful not to mention her source of information. She also managed to track down a visiting film star, and to get Tony to send her to the annual jamboree of irrigation experts; but still he would not let her branch out into hard news, even after she had, reluctantly, sent off as much money as she had earned from Radio Withiel in three weeks as a subscription to the National Union of Journalists.

Tamsin would have liked to dig into what could have been a local scoop. The smuggling of Indian and Pakistani immigrants into Britain by landing them from small boats on the south coast had been a thriving trade for years, though it had never been detected in Cornwall. The present drama arose after the very gale which had preceded Tony Rawe's perfect surf. One of the boats had got into difficulties, and a dinghy-load of six miserable men had beached near Plymouth. Even that would have been almost routine. As it happened, one of the nurses at the hospital at which the six men were treated for exposure and shock before being sent back, in marginally less discomfort, where they had come from, spoke their own language. They told her that their party had originally consisted of eleven men. Five of them were already unwell when the boat left Belgium. The bitter weather conditions had caused the death of at least two of these sufferers, and might have killed another three; the seamen had thrown all five into the sea. Crime of this kind had been reported before from the Arabian Gulf States, into which, as well as Britain, there was a traffic in illegal immigrants, but it was so far unheard of in Europe.

Tony Rawe said that this tragedy was too important and

too delicate for Radio Withiel to tackle. Their audiences wanted background chat; they would not listen to conscience-pricking and harsh reality when they were tuned in for their daily pap. The search for the fishing boat and its crew was being conducted by the international police, the story was being covered by national news agencies, and Tamsin was to keep out of it.

Forbidden hard news, Tamsin suggested a background piece with a retired official of the Home Office immigration department and, as make-weight, an interview with Ivory Judd, who had come back to spend one night with the Buxtons before taking her unsold pictures away. That, Tony agreed, was much more their level.

Tamsin took the children up to River House with her, as it was not a schoolday, and hoped that James would be patient about letting them fiddle with his tools. However, the workshop on the ground floor of the old stone barn was locked, so they all went into the kitchen. Billy was playing with dough, which Anna thought more meaningful than plasticine. She made it with wholemeal flour and coloured it pink with black-currant syrup. Anna seemed very nervous, and kept jumping up and down to fetch food which Ivory refused, like homemade oatcakes, or last year's crab-apple jelly, or some live yoghurt.

Ivory wore an orange wig and purple turban. She did not want herb tea, made by Anna from dried mint leaves, but asked for a glass of cider vinegar diluted with warm water. She smoked heavily scented tobacco in a clay pipe, and emptied its ashes onto the floor with a fine, careless gesture. Pippa and Ben were impressed by her performance, and spent several minutes trying to match the figure before them, swathed in its multicoloured layers of woven fabric, with the glutinously painted flesh on her canvases. It was enough, Ben had told the chaps at school, to put a guy off sex for life. Pippa listened carefully to Ivory's lecture to Anna about releasing herself from the bondage of men and children. Where were the bold, original paintings which Anna should be producing, where the maturation of her early talent? "You should have seen her as a student, Tamsin," Ivory rhapsodised. "Fresh, skilful; and now she's squandering the gods' gift by being a beast of burden."

Ivory referred to a singular deity only when she wished to shock her audience, by using the feminine noun, but evidently she found the concept of a pantheon acceptable. She said that woman had freed herself from the tyranny of the male; she had control over her own body; her fertility was at her own disposal. Pippa wondered whether this had something to do with the notion of the virgin birth.

"It's wonderful to have seen you at home," Ivory declared. "The house. The environment. The babies. I love children. In fact, I've been toying with the idea for myself. If Marvin were cleverer, or Giuseppe better-looking . . . It's one's duty to propagate the species when one has so much to offer."

Ivory owned a converted tractor shed near Land's End. She lived in her studio, or painted in her living room, depending on whom she was showing around. Whatever the label, the establishment consisted of a rectangular enclosure whose walls were covered with many self-portraits and photographs of Ivory Judd. Several monthly magazines had featured it as an example of away-from-it-all perfection. To suit the prospective readership, Ivory appeared with one or other of the men currently in her life, or with both. She often boasted that she was ostracised by her reighbours, who, she said, would like to throw stones after her in the street. She also claimed that the couriers on the coaches which went past her door on their scenic drives around the coast pointed her out as one of the most interesting sights in Penwith. She spoke about the natives of the district in which she had chosen to live as though they had only recently ceased to wear woad.

Ivory talked eagerly into Tamsin's tape recorder about her free, unconstrained life, and her oneness with the primitive forces of cliffs and sea. Then she left, her only luggage being a bulging rush basket. She mentioned her gypsylike progress through life, but reminded Anna to write her a cheque for the pictures which had been sold. Anna stood on her doorstep to wave after the corrugated van, an

Augustus John figure with the baby on her hip and the little boy clutching her full skirt; but her face was drawn and pale. She darted her eyes nervously round the peaceful garden, and jumped when Billy dropped a tin full of building blocks. James came out of the workshop and said, "Has she gone?"

Billy started to bash a brick against Ben's knees. Ben looked despairingly at his mother, not daring to hit back. But why didn't Anna tell Billy to stop it?

"Go and clean out Billy's guinea pigs for him," Tamsin said. "It's nearly time to leave for Granny and Grandpa's."

"But we stayed there last week. Why are we going again?"

"I want to interview Grandpa for the radio."

"He wouldn't talk on a potty little station like Radio Withiel," Pippa said scornfully. Driven by Tamsin's furious glare, she followed the two boys round the corner of the house to the yard, which was occupied by three pens of fertile guinea pigs and the lorry which was the Buxtons' only form of transport, since Granny's old donkey would not cooperate in the shafts of the cart James had made. The lorry used too much petrol to be brought out for any purpose except delivering furniture. Anna walked everywhere. Tamsin was ashamed whenever she saw the stationary lorry, or the burdened Anna, of her own dependence on her Mini, and often wondered whether it would be worth selling it in order to acquire some conservationist virtue of her own. She wished she could be as sure of the rectitude of her own behaviour as the Buxtons were of theirs.

Tamsin's recent life had deprived her of comforting certainties. The London house, the settled bourgeois pattern, the illusion of a happy marriage were benefits, or responsibilities, which she had not questioned—although, in the persons of her fictional heroines, she had pondered over physical and emotional inadequacies. The heroines all spent several chapters in self-loathing. It would be interesting, Tamsin thought suddenly, grasping at the wisp of inspiration, to write a book about someone who was sure of herself, a rural heroine of modern times, like Anna. The earlier books were all set in a big town, and full of descriptions of rainy streets, cockney markets, scarlet buses, and queues at seedy clinics to see indifferent doctors. Could she sustain a narrative in which personalities were stable, and only the environment under threat? Her heart sank at the prospect of the high-minded, ungripping literature into which she would have to research.

Meanwhile, Tamsin was on her way to interview a man who, she told Tony Rawe, had almost unequalled experience of illegal immigration. It would be perverse to waste his reactions; she had promised to keep her questions unemotional.

Sir Arnold Lurie was indulgent about Tamsin's still amateurish handling of her tape recorder, and as ready to speak for it, as he had been, years before, to address his little daughter as a princess or a beggarmaid, depending on what clothes she had found in the dressing-up box, or to agree that she could be a ballet dancer, a champion skater or a riding teacher when she was grown up.

Lady Lurie was just walking into the village when Tamsin arrived, and the children jumped out of the car to go with her.

Tamsin joined her father in the garden, where he was bending over an orange azalea. The perfect grooming of the lawn and rose beds might be exactly like the patch in Richmond over which he had spent weekends for forty years, but this sheltered southern corner gave him scope for growing plants of a lushness he had promised himself for years. It was satisfactory, he told Tamsin, to realise minor ambitions.

"I know it's all very nice," Tamsin said doubtfully. The bungalow could have been the twin of countless others in suburbs all over the country.

"You're forgetting the view," her father said gently. Tamsin lifted her eyes to the far end of the garden; the view, certainly, was unique. She wondered whether she would one day find her own desires down to a beautiful outlook. Brannell had not much more to offer. The little town, or large village, was lived in almost exclusively by retired cou-

ples of sufficient wealth to buy houses there, and sufficient
refinement to be happy in a place which offered no un-
domestic entertainment.

Brannell stood on the southeast-facing hillside, overlook-
ing the point where the River Brann joined the sea. On the
far side of the water was the headland of Grebe. As the
seagull flew, or as the boat sailed, Withiel was only three
miles upriver, but the road between Brannell and Withiel
covered more like six. The river was still navigable up to
Withiel, but was heavily silted and useless for trade. In the
Middle Ages, Withiel had been a port and coinage town;
and indeed, further north still, the creek ended at a quay
which had served until the nineteenth century for unloading coal. The river was not deep, and only small craft
moored near Brannell these days, but they decorated the
view, and their abundance gave comforting evidence of
wealth to ageing doomwatchers like Sir Arnold Lurie. Even
he felt that economic crises had some way to go while there
was still a million pounds' worth of British registered
yachts tied up within sight of his sitting room.

The other charm of Brannell for its retired inhabitants
was the quiet. There were no background noises to disturb
the recording of her father's voice when Tamsin took out
her machine, and he had so much of interest to say that the
time allowed for the brief attention span of the average lis-
tener was not enough for all she wanted to hear.

Sir Arnold Lurie had been much concerned with immigration before he retired from the Home Office, and re-
called other episodes when people seeking streets paved
with gold had suffered dreadful fates. He mentioned a cel-
lar full of starving Indians, discovered (after they had been
locked into it for days, silent for fear of deportation) only
when the smell of one of their number who had died became noticed outside, through the pavement ventilators.
Boat holds had been revealed worse than those in slave
ships, for the slave-trade captains had an interest in delivering their cargo in saleable condition. The recent episode
was by no means the first when castaways had been landed
in a pitiful condition. Sir Arnold knew only what he had

read in the newspapers, but he was able to infer a good deal from his own experience. The cynicism of those who had organised such a journey was appalling. There was no need to speak of the hazards of the sea, for the results were only too clear. The beached dinghy had a bracket for an outboard motor, but no motor; there were three oars left, and perhaps another three had floated away. The boat was painted in camouflage colours, grey and blue, and all identifying marks had been removed. The immigrants had never known the names or seen the faces of the men who had received their money.

"Why are they prepared to risk their lives to get into this country?" Tamsin prompted.

"You must remember from what poor homes these people come. They have been brought up on tales of the wealth of Britain, and of course, by their standards, these legends are true. You'd want to come here too, if your home was a village of mud huts, swept away annually by floods, rebuilt to give shelter from summer heat of a hundred degrees. They count wealth, you know, by possession of articles we throw into our dustbins. And they want to work hard. All most of them hope for is the chance to go home again with a decent nest egg."

"And what are the regulations, exactly, which stop them?"

"They are governed by the Immigration Act of 1971. Unless a person is entitled to a British passport by reason of his nationality at the time the Act was passed, or unless he counts as a 'patrial'—which means that one of his parents or grandparents was British—then he will be subject to the restrictions."

"Sir Arnold," Tamsin said, "we hear this kind of story relating to coloured immigrants, often from the Indian subcontinent." Her father twinkled at her, pleased by her use of professional jargon. "I don't recall any similar items about white immigrants, though the Act presumably applies equally to them—for instance, natives of Canada or New Zealand. Are such people exempted?"

"No, the rules are applied strictly, without regard to race

or colour. There have been many cases of visitors from the
'old Commonwealth' being excluded in exactly the same
way."

"Sir Arnold Lurie, thank you very much."

"Now that your gadget isn't running," he said, "I can say
that in fact, if not in theory, unfortunately, colour does
enter into it. Not that the law applies differently—God for-
bid. No, it's simply that it is so much easier for people to
get away with breaking it if they can merge into the background. Nobody ever notices them."

CHAPTER 6

Councillor Mrs. Lumb always enjoyed making site visits. She liked checking on the sticks and stones of the district her authority administered, and she rejoiced in minutiae like the conditions to be included in planning permissions, the details of closing orders made under the Public Health Acts, and the prosecution of those who had sold buns with foreign bodies among the sultanas.

As she drove along the road to Grebe she admired the fresh scar in the turf where overhead power lines had at last been put underground. She paused at the crossroads to write a reminder to herself in her notebook about the condition of a primary school's playground.

A planning committee site meeting had been scheduled to take place at Grebe in the next week, but Mrs. Lumb had brought an official from the Public Health Department with her—an employee whom she still thought of as a sanitary inspector. She did not feel equal to investigating personally drains, vermin, or noxious effluent.

"Some money here," the young man remarked, as they turned onto Grebe's smooth drive. "This can't be an adopted road."

"Some of the money should have been spent on replanting, then," Mrs. Lumb said, and she pulled up to write, "Tree preservation orders at Grebe, query."

"I was expecting a bigger place than this," the man said, as Mrs. Lumb stopped in front of the house.

"It's a good example of vernacular architecture, I'm told," Mrs. Lumb said unenthusiastically. They walked round to the back of the house. "Very slummy," she remarked. There were meat bones on the grass, and empty, unwashed milk bottles piled in the porch. Weeds almost covered the cobblestones, and Mrs. Lumb's shoe slipped on a heap of rotting vegetables.

Music was thumping from the field, and they could see the brightly coloured tents.

"Lovely place for a holiday."

"Imagine the coast of Cornwall if we let everyone work on that principle," Mrs. Lumb said severely. She counted, and wrote down that there were twelve tents and two dormobiles. A tall man came down to say, "What do you want?"

"Are you Simon Wherry?"

"What if I am?"

"I am Councillor Mrs. Lumb," the lady announced. She pulled her shoulders back and looked sternly up at the bearded man. "I would never have thought it of your father's son. Your poor grandmother must be turning in her grave."

"What are you talking about?"

"I'm talking, young man, about this camp of yours."

The Public Health Inspector wandered off to examine the piles of mouldering garbage. Some heads of long hair poked out from tents, and retreated behind canvas again.

"What about the camp?"

"Didn't you read our letters? You haven't had permission for the camp. This is a saturation area. You aren't allowed to have unauthorised camping. You haven't even applied for a permit, have you?"

"Can't a man do what he likes with his own property? Isn't that a salient feature of English law?"

"You know very well that there are restrictions placed on the use of land, whether by the beneficial owner or anyone else," Mrs. Lumb said.

"What am I supposed to do about it?"

"Apply for permission, for one thing, and get these campers off in the meantime. They can go to legal campsites."

"And if I don't?" he asked, still with a derisive note.

"We shall apply for an injunction and issue an enforcement notice against you."

"Really, Mr. Wherry," the Public Health Inspector said, picking his way briskly through the guy ropes. "This won't do at all. The place is filthy; it must be infested with vermin. Our rodent officer will have to call. It will have to be cleared up. I have powers under the Public Health Acts. I would have thought you would be more careful, for your own sake. Look at those flies. Your visitors are using the hedges as latrines. And where are they drawing their water from?"

"Plenty in the tap over there."

"Over the trough? That's in a disgusting state. You'll have notifiable diseases here if you haven't already. And you are not even on the main water supply; I checked with the Rating Office before we set out. That means your private well will need to be tested before you can supply water to visitors. And your sewage-disposal system too. This place can't have been inspected for years."

"Seen all you want?"

"Yes, thank you, Mr. Wherry, more than enough," he said viciously.

Mrs. Lumb said, "Yes, so have I. I'm extremely disappointed. But there we are. What else can you expect nowadays? Good day, Simon." She waited until the car was out on the main road before speaking again. "I might just check up whether that young man is drawing social security. After all, if those campers are paying for their pitches . . . I'm afraid he's gone thoroughly to the bad."

CHAPTER 7

The dawn air was like water at blood temperature, so mild and still that it made no impact on the skin. The tide rose over the sea grass and mud flats without waves or retreats, a steady pull of water against gravity, its gleaming surface spreading imperceptibly. Birds made the only sounds. There were no houses at the top of the creek, only banks covered with little oak trees and the grass which grew beneath them. At low tide the wide view southwards was an expanse of green, shading to the grey of distant sea and sky; then the trickle of the river would be so narrow that it was only visible from nearby. Now, at high tide, when the water filled the silted channel and reclaimed its once navigable territory, it gleamed as silver and as mysterious as the distant horizon. It could have been bottomless. In reality, it was just deep enough for the passage of a tiny craft. Dinghy sailors would time their excursions to bring them to the abandoned quay when the pub was open. They would tie up to rusty rings in the granite setts and walk along the footpath to drink—boastfully, because to have come by water in a wheel-based world was worth talking about. The proprietor knew the tides, but his customers often ignored his advice and would be forced to push their boats through the retreating stream, knee-deep in mud.

The high tide often left other, unrelated, objects at the top of the creek, sometimes to remove them with the ebb and deposit them on other banks or beaches: driftwood, plastic buckets, milk crates, oil cans, and all varieties of floating detritus.

On this morning, while the dawn mist still embraced the trees, the high tide brought a heavier floating object to nudge against the stone blocks of the quay. The pressure of the stone pushed against one of the pockets of gas which sustained the floating mass, and the tide turned rapidly, so that the little difference in buoyancy and in the depth of the water changed the equation which had brought it up the river. It settled onto the mud, lapped at first by the shallow sea, and at last above the surface, emerging from the slime and reeds, one end dipped in the trickle of fresh water which was the origin of this estuarine river.

A dog might have found the body, or a farmer, or a bird watcher perhaps—an ex-soldier inured to death, now addressing his ferocity to the protection of wildfowl.

It was a boy who came joyfully to the quay on this morning. He thought he was knowledgeable and experienced, and that, from watching television, he knew about mortality. He never mistook two dimensions for three again.

Tamsin encouraged the freedom which her children were gradually learning to enjoy. Her idea of a country childhood was that they should disappear for long days with sandwiches and apples in their pockets. She would not complain about dirt, scratches or lateness. What she minded, she often told them, was for them to sit watching a small screen in a stuffy room when a perfect calf country lay outside the door.

That morning she had not heard Ben stealing out of the house, nor stirred when he opened the shed door to get his bike and ride off to adventure. She woke when he came stumbling back, and went down to find him muddy and dishevelled, wearing his pyjama top under his pullover, with his sheath knife attached to his belt, and a motorcyclist's crash helmet on his head. Wet channels made by tears shone on his pale face. The scolding died on her lips.

"Darling, what's wrong? Aren't you feeling well? Here—" She put out her hand to test the temperature of his forehead, but he pushed it aside. His voice was hoarse, and all she could make out was, "Mummy, please come. You must come." He pulled her by the cloth of her nightdress.

"I must put some clothes on, then," she said calmly, try-

ing to impose rational behaviour by example. She knew
that Ben was inarticulate when he was upset; long experience had taught her that she would have to go to see what
he was unable to describe—a puncture, perhaps, or an
angry farmer who needed a mother's word for the fact that
this boy always closed field gates and kept his feet off
standing crops.

"Come on, Mummy," he wailed, as she came down, still
buckling her belt over an oiled wool jersey. "Come on."

"Which way shall I go?" she asked, hands waiting on the
steering wheel, and he directed her with a gesture. "I hope
this won't take too long, Ben. If we're not back when Pippa
wakes up, she'll be worried." Ben told her to stop the car,
not far beyond a little pub, and he led her, clutching at her
sleeve, over a stile and along a short path. She could smell
the sea and mud, and hear the birds' cries.

"There," Ben uttered hoarsely. "I can't look."

Tamsin could not look, either, after her first glance at the
heap of muddy rags and her second, in the nature of a
double take, when her sluggish brain interpreted the message of her eyes.

She rushed back to Ben, who was crouched shivering on
the ground with his hands over his ears, and hugged him
very tightly, burying her face in the back of his neck. For a
moment it was she who needed the comfort of his warm
proximity.

A body: that was all. It sounded so simple. A human
body. There must be so many of them, as many as ever
there were people. But Tamsin had never seen one before,
and reason asserted that not many would have seen a body
in the state of this one. The smell! The shapelessness! The
unspeakable tatters of— Better, surely, not to consider of
what those seaweedlike pieces of fibre, now unsupported
by water, consisted. And the gleaming white she had noticed before jerking her gaze away, which must be—stop it.

Tamsin took several deep breaths and stood up, holding
Ben's hand firmly. Neither of them would stay on guard.
What further harm could befall that sad object? Even if
there were the likelihood of predators, nothing would per-

suade her to stay there any longer, or consider letting Ben do so.

A telephone box stood outside the pub, but the cord had been torn from the wall and the glass in the windowpanes broken, and the floor was awash with urine. Tamsin looked up at the curtained windows of the public house and the two cottages which were all that stood in this hamlet. The main part of the village was nearly a mile in the opposite direction from Withiel, and Withiel itself not more than ten minutes' drive away. She pushed Ben back into the car.

Think, Tamsin. Where is the police station? While you change gear and steer round these narrow curves and return your left hand to hold Ben's right, and make him feel that with you beside him nothing dreadful can happen, visualise the streets of Withiel. Is there a blue illuminated sign reading POLICE in the main road? Or down one of the alleys? No, it suddenly came to Tamsin, as she reached the traffic lights on the edge of the town, and she was able to drive directly to the steep hill called Brannell Road, at the top of which a modern police headquarters had recently been opened.

They were very kind, with the quick and practical kindness of efficient, worldly men. They agreed that there was no need for her to go back to the quay; they could see that the little boy had had a nasty shock. Take him home and give him hot, sweet tea, they said, and they would call round later and have a word with him. Yes, they knew exactly where she lived. That would all, they said credibly, be quite all right; and the power of their massive calm got her back to the cottage, and enabled her to praise Ben for his good sense and scold Pippa for having been in a panic when she woke to find herself alone. Tamsin fetched the electric heater to create a cosy fug, and fed Ben on soothing milkshakes and pancakes so that the familiar food of teatime treats would reinforce the consolations of home. When she looked out of the window she was astonished to realise that it was not yet nine o'clock, and the morning sun was shining into the east window of the sitting room. There was a long day to live through.

There would be photographers, she thought. The police would erect a shelter, and send for experts in fingerprints and pathology. She dredged her memory for the procedure described in a sort of fiction which had not interested her in the past, since she had always believed it to treat of matters far removed from normal life and normal people.

I suppose somebody has to find bodies, Tamsin told herself. There is no reason why the Oriel family should be immune. But then she admonished herself, not to let it go to her head. Everyday life would not be transformed into melodrama on account of finding a pathetic corpse, from a world that her own would never cross.

Nor, she thought, must Ben be allowed to make too much of all this. He must be treated with the same lack of emotion which Tamsin had already rehearsed for Pippa's expected, but unrealised, encounter with a "flasher" or other "nasty man."

No visitor from the police appeared until nearly the end of a long, long morning. Sir Arnold and Lady Lurie would come later, but her father said that Ben must wait until he had given an account of his experience to the authorities. Sir Arnold said, with unexpected severity, that Ben was quite old and sensible enough to do that. Think what nine-year-old boys in city slums had to cope with. Think of nineteenth-century children, no older than Ben, taking over the care of their orphaned siblings. He asked quickly, and rang off as though he regretted the question, whether the body had been that of a coloured man.

Pippa added her mite to the attack on Tamsin's self-pity. "I thought you always said there was nothing dreadful about dying, Mummy. You always told us that everyone dies. You said that it can't be awful if it happens to every single person that's born. Didn't you, Mummy? Mummy, didn't you say—?"

"Shut up, Pip," Ben said gruffly. And Tamsin could only answer that it was not quite the same thing, and please, Pippa, shut up because Mummy had a headache.

It was all very well to have brought the children up on what she now realised was a comfortable rationalisation of a fear she had never had to face. Nobody for whom Tamsin cared had died yet. But the reality of death did not seem to match her comfortable theory. What she had seen that morning was more horrible, surely, than a discarded husk which had not been tidied away in the usual manner.

The pink-faced juvenile constable, who came with the older police sergeant, must have had far greater experience of reality than she, Tamsin thought. And she wondered how she had dared to suppose she was writing about humans and their emotions. She knew nothing, she realised. She had skated on the surface of civilisation, protected from suffering and crisis.

CHAPTER 8

The inquest was adjourned by the Coroner, Mr. Lumb, to await further evidence. All that was revealed at the brief hearing was that the body was that of a Caucasian man, probably between the ages of twenty and forty, who had died before entering the water, since there was no seawater in the lungs. The pathologist said that it was likely he had been suffocated as a result of oedema of the glottis and larynx, but he intended to make further investigations, and the police also wanted to pursue other lines of enquiry in order to identify the corpse. One thing was certain: the body was not that of one of the murdered Pakistani or Indian immigrants.

Tamsin found it both disconcerting and galling to know as little as any other member of the public about the case. She felt a proprietary interest in it, and chafed at being excluded from the solution of a problem which she and her son had been instrumental in posing. She wondered whether a local farmer or bird watcher would have been told more, had he been the one to find the body. Was she being kept out because she was a woman, or a foreigner, or perhaps because she might give secrets away to Radio Withiel?

The event, which seemed of major significance to her, raised little national interest, and even in the locality the buzz was subdued. All right, perhaps it was commonplace to die out of bed. It was happening all the time in Northern Ireland, on the roads—all over the world, in fact. But Tamsin could not believe that the pathos of the corpse she had seen was typical or common. Surely nobody—not the most experienced of pathologists—could have seen it unmoved?

She found herself, from time to time, looking at her own flesh, visualising the state to which seawater could transform it, and guiltily snapping her eyes away, as though Ben could read her thoughts. He seemed to have forgotten the horror, and to remember only that it had brought him attention—from the policemen who came to the cottage; from friends and teachers at school; and, briefly, from the local press. Pippa was the more affected of the two children by the thought of the dead man, although she had not seen him.

In detective novels—and Tamsin had read as many as she could find since being plunged into the kind of circumstances in which they specialised—the *dramatis personae* always seemed to be more actively involved with the police investigations and kept up with what was going on; the police officer, in a gentlemanly way, gave them progress reports. Was that all a figment of novelists' imaginations? Tamsin suspected that the convention was as unreal as her own perceptions of human nature were beginning to seem.

Fictional detectives seemed to be, variously, lugubrious middle-aged men of limited intuition and dogged perseverance; or men, equally advanced in years but described as young, who had the education of scholars, the sensitivity of artists, the insights of psychiatrists, and behaviour so civilised as to be obliged from time to time to remind their suspects that they were not gentlemen but players. Both varieties had faithful subordinates who admired when they did not adore their bosses. All made lists of clues, allowed amateur assistants to listen to their conversations with witnesses, and held gatherings of participants at the end of which one stood revealed as the culprit. The victim's death was often described in graphic and repulsive terms, but only servants, or their modern equivalent, were permitted to say that they had been affected by the sight. Less farcical characters were evidently immune from the disconcerting emotions from which Tamsin had not yet recovered. She felt that the whole world around her had lurched into a different gear.

Yet external life carried on as a different kind of fiction

specified: the sun shone on a flower-sprinkled countryside, newly painted boats arrived at their summer moorings, the air smelt of mown grass and honey-heavy gardens. Domestic life was easier than Tamsin had ever known it; not only was she without a man—and a demanding one at that—to cater for, but also, with neither the children nor herself wearing socks or stockings, vests or jerseys, or eating hot food, she could almost forget about cooking and washing and the perpetual little cares which had always crowded her life.

Anna, however, was finding life more, and not less, difficult. Tamsin could diagnose at a glance that Anna Buxton was suffering severely from postnatal depression. It was a textbook case: Emmy was four months old; Bill was at an age to be as boring as a death-watch beetle; Anna's image of herself as a mother precluded the admission that she did not find perfect happiness in her children's company. Tamsin could remember days when little tears had squeezed out of her eyes from yawning as she looked after Pippa and Ben, listening, reading, playing, filling in the time until they could be put to bed. She used to say that nature's way of making mothers bear the soul-destroying tedium was by giving them the illusion that their own toddling infants were the sweetest the world had ever seen.

Anna did not boast of Billy and Emmy's unique charm, and perhaps it was because she could not admit her own passion, she could not cope with its disappointments. Her milk had failed, and Emmy had to be fed from a bottle. James had bought an ill-tempered nanny goat, so that she would be spared the indignity of working out formulae, but every time she saw the glass and rubber she flinched from it.

"It's unnatural. I can't bear the smell," she said fiercely.

"Caesarian operations and vaccination aren't natural, either."

"Those are for emergencies. Breast-feeding, it's like natural childbirth—it's a right which only a sick civilisation denies."

"Nature's way is to cull the human race with perinatal

mortality and puerperal fever, and leave only the fittest to survive."

Anna would not listen. She was shrouded in a cocoon of misery. It seemed a pity that James, so kind and helpful, could not be a little more cheerful himself, and snap Anna out of her gloom. Tamsin felt obliged to play the part of the good neighbour. She made herself be brisk and jolly and efficient—the sort of woman, in fact, that in Alexander's eyes she had been.

Was her idea of her husband equally ill-judged? Tamsin's mental picture of Alex was of a man in a dark room: a restaurant; or their living room, which was so carefully fitted with tasteful lamps that reading and sewing were almost impossible; or in his own office, with the lights turned out, as he left it for the theatre or the opera. Her memories of him were set indoors: pouring wine into a decanter with steady movements of his long white fingers; balancing a record between those delicate palms as he searched its grooves for scratches; walking round a gallery of fashionable paintings with a reserved, cautious expression on his face; standing dutifully, doggedly, on the soft carpet of a dress department while she paraded for him to choose the garment which best suited, not her image, but his.

She was startled, therefore, at the weekend to see Alex on the cottage doorstep, in the sun, with faint beads of sweat on his forehead. He said that he had tried to telephone her several times. The bell had sounded, she remembered, when she had decided not to leave her sunbathing and answer it. Once, passing it on her way out, she had lifted the receiver to hear a girl say, "Mrs. Oriel? Hold the line, please. I have Mr. Oriel for you." Gently Tamsin had replaced the receiver on its rest. She wondered whether she would have accepted Mr. Oriel gift-wrapped; the telephonist's phrase was double-edged. Alex, of all people, should have known that Tamsin would not hold on to speak to him, or anyone else, so that he could be disturbed less than she was; she would not pander to the treatment of secretaries' bosses as little tin gods.

He must have told the people at his office that she was

on holiday. "Her parents have retired to Cornwall and she's helping to settle them in," he would have said. "Sir Arnold Lurie, you may know him. Yes, it is lonely, but I'm managing." His directors, shark-faced and experienced, would make polite sounds to indicate that they neither believed him nor thought he expected them to believe what he had said. But convention would be observed until the new-model wife was unveiled; like a car, Tamsin thought, at the Motor Show, Clarissa would be displayed in her pristine, expensive gloss.

So Alex turned up unannounced. He wore new resort clothes in impeccable taste. He was tanned, and had come in an open sports car. He stooped under the doorway to enter the cottage, and came into the kitchen. His head scraped the ceiling, his shoulder brushed against the dangling string of onions, and his nose wrinkled at the mess and the smell, not only of breakfast but of several preceding meals also. Tamsin cleared up only to please herself, and often chose leisure rather than order. Her appearance had changed too; she was wearing clothes he would not have allowed, neither so shabby and dirty that she was obviously about to change, nor so elegantly casual that he would have said they were just the thing for country weekends. He had precise notions about the images presented by his family, and Tamsin, looking merely dowdy, did not fit them. Aloud, he remarked, "You've put on weight."

Tamsin put the kettle on the stove, which was scattered with grains of dried-up rice and shrivelled peas, and rinsed out a cup.

"I won't offer you one. I know you don't like instant coffee."

"I wouldn't have thought you did, either."

"Wouldn't you?" She stirred the powder and water together, and ostentatiously spooned some sugar into the mixture. She saw Alex push a crust of bread under the table with the toe of his brightly white tennis shoes. He brushed the crumbs off Ben's stool and perched on its edge.

"This is the simple life with a vengeance," he said. "Do you really like it?"

"I have changed. I have had to change."

"Oh, Lord, don't start recriminating again." He nibbled at grains of sugared wheat cereal.

"How is Clarissa?" Tamsin asked formally.

"Oh, fine, thanks, in very good form. She thinks Cornwall is lovely, so far. We spent the night down at St. Mawes. But she's terribly tired, poor girl. London is awful in this weather. You don't know your luck to be down here instead."

"I can't imagine," Tamsin said slowly, "how I came to marry such an insensitive man as you in the first place. Have you always been like this?"

But she thought that he had not always been as he now was; not when they were young, and he had not succumbed to the lures of luxury. Or perhaps she herself had changed, for she could not remember that she had objected to dressing carefully and observing the forms Alex thought proper.

"Where are the children?" he asked. "I thought I'd take them out to lunch."

"How will you explain Clarissa to them?"

"They are too young to ask questions. But they'll have to be told sometime. What have you said?"

"Hardly anything."

"No sly little comments? No hints? That isn't like you."

"A year ago I'd have said it wasn't like you to leave me and the children for a girl half your age."

"*Touché*. But, when you wonder why I did, you might search your own conscience. Clarissa enters into my interests; she really cares about my work, which is more than you did."

"And more than you did for my work, come to that."

"That's different. I'm the breadwinner. Anyway, I got pretty damned sick of your veiled comments about people who are sweating their guts out to make money so that more sensitive mortals can cultivate their souls. It's not even as though you really appreciated the things I provided. You turned into such a damned puritan. All that fuss about not needing new clothes, or not wanting to redecorate the drawing room before the Weissweillers came to dinner. Clarissa knows how the wife of a successful man is supposed to behave."

"So you want to marry her."

"That's another thing we must talk about."

"Not now. Come on, we'll walk up to find the children."

What gulfs of incomprehension could be left between two articulate people. Tamsin thought of how she had guarded Alex's money because she never knew how much he had; all the while, he evidently had interpreted her reluctance to spend as the ungracious behaviour of a professional killjoy. How was she to know, after all, since when they were first married they were poor, and after Pippa's birth poorer? He might have told her what he was earning; that he never did was further witness to the fact that he recognised her existence only in the light of his own. But until Clarissa came into their lives, Tamsin had no idea of the falsity of the relationship between herself and Alex. She had truly believed them to be a united couple, and truly accepted his picture of her rôle as the wife of a young executive. He might have been better satisfied if she had been acting.

"How are the children getting on at school?" Alex enquired politely. "Their letters are all about children I've never heard of being quite well."

"They seem happy," Tamsin said.

"I don't see how Ben will ever get into a decent public school. We'll have to send them to prep schools if you aren't moving back to London."

"Do you want me to move back to London? What about—?"

"I shan't be there. You must do as you like. I did tell you that there was a chance I might go to the States, and they have offered me the transfer. Clarissa's keen."

"Big of you to tell me."

"Sarcasm never did suit you. Anyway, we'll have to decide about the house. Can you find yourself a solicitor? Nigel will naturally be acting for me."

"If I don't agree to divorce you, it will take you another

four and a half years." Tamsin could not bring herself to voice her malicious thought: that by then Clarissa would not have the same appeal for him. He nodded, and she cried, "How can you bear to be so banal? You're like a cartoon, or a character in a revue. Chucking me and the children for Clarissa! What will you do when it's her turn to be thirty-two and tied down by your children? Trade her in for the third Mrs. Oriel?"

"We'd better not quarrel," he said with a certain dignity. "Not just when I'm going to see Pippa and Ben." He stalked on beside her, his elongated shadow falling familiarly on the ground beside her own. Suddenly, now that Alex was beside her, Tamsin was freed from her long hatred of Clarissa. Momentarily, she felt almost sorry for the pretty, affected creature; what a lifetime of working at slickness and elegance lay before her.

"This is River House where the Buxtons live. They are my landlords."

"Can you bear their way of life? It's a pretty good slum," he said, looking distastefully at the outside of River House. Tamsin noticed, really for the first time, the details which to him must be highlighted, not so much of a mess, but of general seediness. When the day was busy from dawn till dusk with laborious cultivation and handworked imitations of what a machine could make in a fraction of the time, it was natural to neglect the cosmetic touches which Alex would require.

"It's fantastically hard work, living like this," Tamsin told him. "They do pretty well everything themselves, by hand. And they have such disasters. Mice eat through the potatoes they've stored for the winter, or the slugs get the whole cabbage crop. It's all two steps forward and one step back."

"It has the same air of moral earnestness," Alex said, "as the curate's house my Uncle Ninian lived in before he got his parish. Grace and porridge."

They walked round the house to the old barn. The sliding doors to the workshop were half-open, and they saw James working at his bench, planing a piece of wood with strong, steady movements of his arm. Ben stood beside him, catching the shavings, and Pippa was polishing linseed oil into the flank of a rocking horse.

"Daddy," they shouted together. They rushed at Alex and fought to hug him, but he soon pushed Pippa's hands off and brushed at the oily mark she had left on his shirt.

"If you two scoot back to the cottage and change, I'll take you out to lunch."

"Mummy, must we change?" they chorused. Tamsin shrugged her shoulders and went to look at James's work. Behind her she heard Alex being firm; no doubt it was important to him that Clarissa should be impressed by her future stepchildren's charm. Tamsin slammed the window in her mind which showed a vista of a court giving custody, care and control of Pippa and Ben to their mother, and herself denying Alex access to them.

"James," she said. "You haven't met my—you haven't met Alexander Oriel." James turned and held out his hand, and Alex hesitated only briefly before shaking it.

"You and your wife are very good to my family, I hear," he said, flicking his eyes around the untidy, unprosperous workshop.

"Come and meet Anna," James said with relief. He was never good at formalities.

Alex looked even less enthusiastic, if possible, about the inside of the house. Anna was surrounded by disorder; leaking paper packets of wheat germ and vitamins, sticky pots of molasses and yeast extract, unwashed unfinished bottles of goat's milk, and numerous half-eaten apples and oatmeal biscuits scattered by Billy.

Alex liked a kitchen to display bread crocks and butter moulds on an antique pine dresser, and copper pans on the tiled wall, but he expected them to produce, from an elaborate *batterie de cuisine*, sophisticated meals. Anna's enamel and oilcloth surfaces, littered with the evidence of the simple life which was mocked by Tamsin's expensive London kitchen, clearly seemed deplorable to him. Anna was in her stained dressing gown, and Billy and Emmy were both whining. As much for her sake as Alex's, Tamsin led him away at once.

They returned to the cottage to find the children in their underpants with every garment they possessed laid out for Alex to choose from. When they left, they looked like the ideal Sunday supplement family getting out of Mum's way while she cooked Sunday lunch.

Tamsin wished Clarissa joy of them. She spent the day scribbling a short story, writing out of herself her irrational jealousy. She truly no longer grudged Alex to Clarissa; she did not want to be, any longer, a living advertisement of his financial acumen. She did not enjoy his company anymore. She wished that she had been the one to take the initiative, because it was embarrassing to be cast in the rôle of the deserted wife, but she knew it was not the taste of sour grapes which enabled her to confess that she had been living a false life. It was about time that she rebelled against being a drone in an industrial beehive.

To accept that a previous life was over was one thing. To welcome the alternative offered by her new associates was quite another. Tamsin had a long way to go before she could face the toil and sweat of self-sufficiency. Indeed, after the reminder of sophistication from Alex, she had to force compassion to overcome irritation, and go back to River House the next day, and the next, and the one after that, on day after cloudless day, when the drink and the deck chair on the lawn were hard to resist. Instead, Tamsin received visitors in the gallery, and hung washed nappies on the line, and took the babies for walks, leaving Anna hunched over an empty hearth, weeping.

On the towpath one day, while Tamsin was trying to interest Bill in the birds and his only concern was to force grass into Emmy's mouth, Tamsin decided to buy her children a boat. In her own mind the river was still associated with death, and if Pippa and Ben were concealing a similar revolting obsession, it should be exorcised at once. It would be the equivalent of climbing back on a horse immediately after taking a toss.

"Perhaps you should get out in your boat more," she

suggested to Anna when she returned the children to River House. The Buxtons' little motor cruiser was moored not far from the *Cock's Comb,* but Tamsin hardly ever saw James rowing out to it. Bill started to shout, "Boat, boat," and ran violently around the room in the undirected manner which Tamsin found most disconcerting. She had not put into words her fear that the child was already marked down as one who would grow up to be unstable, but she thought his behaviour incomprehensibly erratic.

"I never want to set foot in another boat so long as I live," Anna said violently.

"Oh why? Did you ever—?"

"I just don't. You wouldn't understand," she said. She shuffled over to the cooker and started to stir some mess of simmering pulses. She did not get dressed these days, and was wearing a stained and spotted dressing gown made of undyed linen, and her normally smooth hair was uncombed and greasy. She glanced nervously at the window from time to time, and then put the spoon down and went to pull the blind down.

"Is it too sunny for you?" Tamsin asked.

"I don't want people to see in."

"Who could? This only looks out onto your garden."

James shook his head behind Anna's back, and made a "leave it" gesture. Tamsin wondered whether she could persuade James to bring his mother down from the Midlands for a few weeks. All this was really getting too much. Surely there must be some relation of Anna's who could cope?

When Anna had gone to bed, which she had taken to doing at intervals during the day, Tamsin said firmly, "You can't go on like this, James. You'll have to get someone in. Who is your doctor?"

"Anna won't see him. She says she isn't ill. I don't think she is, either—just sad about not being able to feed the baby, and overtired. We don't believe in drugs, so there isn't much a doctor could do except tell her to rest."

"What's this about people looking in at the window?"

"Anna thought there was a face at the glass the other evening. I couldn't find anyone."

"I think you'll have to do something soon," Tamsin repeated. "I shan't be able to help so much once my children are on holiday. Anyway, I'll come tomorrow and take Billy and Emmy for a walk again," she said, with a faint sigh.

At breakfast the next morning Pippa and Ben protested at the chaos Bill had made in their belongings, and watched her, beady-eyed, while she cleared Pippa's flower press and weaving loom, and Ben's Action Man outfit, onto shelves which even the hyperactive Bill could not reach. Her own typewriter had been in its case for days.

James met Tamsin in the stable yard, looking embarrassed.

"It's awfully sweet of you," he said. "Actually, Anna wants to keep the children with her. She doesn't want them to go out."

Tamsin went in to find Anna, dressed and looking more organised.

"I want them with me," she said.

"It's a lovely day again. Why don't you get some fresh air?"

"We're staying here."

"Do you want me to give Bill a lift to his playgroup this afternoon?"

"Not today, thanks."

Tamsin shrugged her shoulders, not sorry to have the chance to get some of her own work done, but feeling irrationally annoyed with Anna all the same. She had plenty of interviews to plan. She was booked to chat with a visiting violinist, a man whose dog barked in time to his accordion, and a woman who had modelled Truro Cathedral out of yoghurt cartons. The next day she was to go out on a fishing boat and get material for a longer programme which Tony Rawe hoped to sell to a national network. Tamsin also had one or two ideas for short stories, even if not for the long book which she hoped would soon bubble out of her subconscious. She rather looked forward to sitting down and working out some witty paragraphs about the lives of those who lived in the modern version of Cold Comfort Farm.

James caught her up as she was walking down the drive.

"I wanted to ask what you thought about Anna today," he said.

"She seems better, doesn't she?"

"I don't know. Did she say anything to you about moving away?"

"No, of course not. I should think she would have to be quite out of her mind to think of that."

"She says she doesn't feel safe. It's something to do with that time she thought she saw a man in the garden. She seems to think the children might be abducted or something."

"Are you rich enough to be worth a kidnapper's while?"

"I haven't any money at all. What we have is Anna's, but it's all gone on the house and so on."

"You'll have to get someone to see Anna, James. You know, women do get these obsessions after having babies. It can be treated."

"She says that if I won't come with her she will simply take the children and go. What am I to do if she won't see a doctor, Tamsin? I can't keep her prisoner. What shall I do if one day I find she's gone?"

CHAPTER 9

The other time she had run away it was raining; she had
T. S. Eliot's words in her mind: "A cold coming we had of
it,/Just the worst time of year/For a journey." Then she'd
been going toward a better life.

Anna dressed in unnoticeable clothes, jeans, here where
holidaymakers wore them as a uniform. They would not
meet round her waist, but she fastened them with a nappy
pin and put a cheesecloth smock on top, so as to look either
fat or pregnant, but not remarkable either way. She
combed her hair, like blinkers, down over her cheeks.

Bill whined as they walked into town. She had taken the
carry-cot on its wheeled transporter, and the contraption
would not bear Bill's weight. She jollied him along.

It was all right on the footpaths through the alleys and
opes. Nobody gave a second glance to a mother with her
kids. But she did not want to cross the main road, clogged
as it always was with dawdling people and cars.

They went past the church hall where Bill attended playgroup three days a week, and she had to quieten his wails
because they did not go in. She had enjoyed the happy
nondescript normality of waiting with the other mothers in
that lobby for the story and songs to finish, talking about
toy fairs and festivals of sand castles, and which of the
local primary schools the children would go on to.

They went in at the side door of the church, and tiptoed
down the aisle and out into the front porch. She waited beside the lists of electors, dates of forthcoming services and
notices about flower-arranging rotas. There was a warning
that no member of the Church of South India would be admitted to Communion.

The traffic had come to a seemingly permanent halt in the main road outside. Two coaches of holidaymakers had met at the very point where the driver of a juggernaut lorry was unloading crates of bananas. Anna squinted from the shelter of the porch at the drivers within sight. She knew one; he was a father who fetched his child from playgroup. Behind him queued two harmless-looking women with cars full of kids, and a milk roundsman. She clamped Bill's hand under hers on the handlebar, and made a dash for it, keeping her head low and steering the pram down the path, under the lych gate, between the waiting cars and up the steps into the post office. She watched again as the traffic started to edge forward, but at this time of year, with so many strangers about, knew it would be hard to pick out an individual.

She rang for a taxi from the telephone booth, and when it came she was ready with the carry-cot in one hand and the folded transporter in the other. Bill was holding tightly to her clothes, awed to silence by her strange behaviour, and she was able to get them into the taxi quickly and direct the driver to take her to the railway station in Truro.

"It'll cost you, lady," he said, with a dubious glance in his mirror.

"I can pay. Look." She held out a bank note over the seat.

Twenty miles to the station. It was not the nearest, but all the trains stopped there. She wondered how far to go, along the one railway line out of the county. Bill was quiet now, pleased at first to be in a proper car, and later lulled to drowsiness by the noise of the engine and the heat. Emmy slept angelically, her small fist half in her open mouth.

As the car passed through villages and farmland, woods and valleys, Anna thought, as she often had before, that it was a good countryside, the right environment for mankind; small-scale but mysterious, inhabited but not over-populated. In the old days Anna had imagined landscapes very like this. When she had first set eyes on Withiel and

Grebe, she had said to herself: This is it. This is the place to live and bring up children.

It was for this she had taken her dowry; for this domestic land, and the chance to grow on it the food they would eat, and to live in a way which was neither harmful nor exposed to harm.

Anna had believed that she had come to her spiritual home. She would not be kicked around anymore like a football, at other people's whim. But here she was again, harried into flight.

Someone up there, she thought, is out to get me. A malign fate watches over me.

She had never thought she would be tracked down in Withiel, though the fear of it was only thinly buried in her mind. But bogeymen should not turn into faces seen in Withiel's main street, or at the windows of her own house. If only she could believe that she had projected a mental image onto a harmless base, distorting the face of a harmless tourist, or a branch knocking at the windows of River House. Anna hugged Billy closer to her, and tried to convince herself that she was fleeing from imaginary fears.

I'm suffering from postnatal depression, that's all, she thought. Things are getting on top of me. But she knew very well, from seeing James in his bad patches, that one could recognise one's depression as unfounded and unreasonable, watch oneself weeping and moping and making family life miserable, and still not be able to stop. If she went back, she would still see faces at the window. And if they were real after all . . .

Anna had not been to Truro Station since her first weeks in Cornwall. Bill had been in the carry-cot then, and James at her side. He was going to collect his belongings from his flat, and his tools from the school—not that many of them were left undamaged to collect, by the time he got there, weeks after the beginning of term. James had gone straight from Paddington Station to Liverpool Street, to catch a train which would let him get back to her the same evening. Anna said she would go to a friend, and he left her standing in the taxi queue. She had driven straight to Som-

erset House, knowing of it only from reading novels, and
was almost surprised when it was indeed the centre for records of birth, marriages and deaths. They had not even
minded when she left the baby in his cot, in the imposing
entrance hall. The porter offered to keep an eye on him,
but the baby had just been fed and would sleep for a
while. Anyway, the porter said, if he cried she would hear
it resounding through the building.

In those days Anna was not used to kindness from
officials, and looked at the man dubiously, wondering
whether he might have an ulterior motive; but eventually
she thanked him, made some unnecessary adjustment to the
baby's covering and went into the office. She knew exactly
what she planned to do, and had decided on alternative
methods in case she could not manage the first; but she
found what was necessary with very little difficulty, and
nobody asked why she wanted to look through the volumes
of registers of deaths for 1950, and of births for the two
years before that.

Anna had ordered exactly what she needed before Billy
even stirred: the birth certificate of Anne Grace Cook,
daughter of Edwin and Adelaide Cook, who were then living at Freeman's Buildings, Rotherham. Anne Grace Cook
had been born on 16 May 1949; and the death certificate,
which Anna did not bespeak, would have stated that she
died on 4 August 1950, from infantile paralysis. Even the
initials matched, though that was an irrelevant detail; Anna
Grete Cohen, for all official purposes, was to lose her identity in that of a long-dead child. While she waited for the
document, Anna wondered why nobody marked the deaths
into the birth registers. Other people might embark on
frauds far more harmful than the one Anna was about to
undertake.

The armour of carrying a birth certificate of a native-
born citizen changed one's whole attitude, Anna found. She
felt no qualm, and hardly any fear, while she sat in the
booth at Oxford Circus Underground station waiting for
the coin-in-the-slot camera to produce her photograph, but,
rather, a calm satisfaction as she stared into the mirror, or

watched legs and feet passing on the other side of the short green curtain. She put another coin into the slot and took a set of pictures of herself and Billy, just for the pleasure of seeing his tiny face against hers. She liked the sight of the row of four eyes as she pressed their cheeks together, and the amusing likeness of his miniature mouth to hers. Once she had the photographs, she took a taxi to the main passport office; taxis were another pleasant and unfamiliar experience for her.

It came as a slight shock to find that it was necessary for the photograph to be attested by a person who had known her for two years and whose probity was shown by his profession. What if she did not know anyone like that? she had asked the girl behind the counter.

"There must be someone. Everyone manages. Haven't you got a doctor, or a solicitor? Or what about the head of your old school?" Anna did not argue, but withdrew with the form. She went to Kensington Gardens, because she had read about them and never been there, and sat on a bench beside the Round Pond to feed Billy and eat her own lunch of fruit and cheese. This obstacle, smaller than those she had feared to encounter, would not stop her now. Perhaps she could ask one of the strangers sitting nearby to write his name; there was one gentleman in a bowler and pinstripes who was surely a pillar of the community. Then it occurred to her that it would not be hard to find a professional man who would sign the form for the sake of what she could pay him, without asking too many questions. Or she could simply write down the name of a solicitor or doctor; but would he have a rubber stamp to prove his identity? She did not want to have one made, though that would be easy also.

An elected councillor would not have an official stamp; not, at least, any of those whom Anna had known. She fished about in her memory for a name. It was surely a safe gamble to bet that hers would not be the one random application to have its reference examined. If there was cause to investigate more deeply than the birth certificate and referee's address, a forged signature would be the least of her worries.

Alderman Payne. She remembered his name suddenly, perhaps because he had caused her plenty of suffering. Albert Payne; a self-important, fat, red-faced butcher, with no time for girls whose husbands had disappeared, if—which he took leave to doubt—they had ever existed in the first place. He was on the Supplementary Benefits Tribunal, the Housing Committee, the Hospital Board, and virtually every other organisation which gave him scope for ungenerous interference. He said, displaying unexpected historical knowledge, that he would have been the first in the good old days of the Poor Laws to move the indigent on to the next parish. He didn't pay rates, or administer them, to support in luxury the bastards of girls who were no better than they should be. This stand had been very popular with the section of the electorate which bothered to vote in local polls.

It was a pretty safe guess that Alderman Payne was still there behind his marble counter, meeting, as he often said in his speeches, all kinds and conditions of people, who came in and told him their troubles, he implied, even if they could not afford to buy his meat.

Anna wrote, in a mean, uneducated handwriting, "Albert Payne, Councillor," underlined the words with a showy flourish suitable for so vain a man, and put under it the address of his butcher's shop. She could see it now, reeking and gleaming with dead, unplucked birds hanging in a row from the window frame. At that time she had been a vegetarian only because she could not afford meat, but the memory was enough to make any carnivore puke.

She wrote her borrowed name on the back of the photograph and clipped it to the form. She carried Billy through the park to a post office, bought an envelope, postal order and stamp, and sent it all off.

And that had been that. Ten days later, Anne Grace Cook collected from the *poste restante* at Truro Post Office a glossy, dark-blue booklet which should confer freedom not only of the wide world, but also of the British Citizens

entry channel at British ports and airports. Three weeks
later, Anna Cook and James Buxton had gone through a
ceremony of marriage at the registry office in Withiel. The
registrar was a friendly woman who remembered James's
grandmother; the little office was decorated with roses from
the wedding before theirs. It did not seem likely that anyone would think to ask how a child whose death had been
recorded in 1950 had contracted a marriage in 1974. Anna
had never used Anne Grace Cook's passport, and she and
James had no wish to travel, but she had handed in the virgin passport and acquired another in the name of Anne
Grace Buxton, and treasured it, and the birth certificate,
and the certificate of her marriage to James, as her proof, in
a way, that she existed at all.

Even today, two years later, the shivering, desperate
creature who had realised that she must run away again
had packed her precious evidence; the passport and the
certificates lay beside a cheque-book and a pile of clean
nappies, and a collection of clean clothes, and polythene
bags to put the dirty ones in, under the mattress of the
carry-cot. Anna would not want for much that money could
buy.

She paid off the taxi driver in the forecourt of Truro Station, and one of the men who was leaning against the wall
in the sun came forward to help her unfold the wheels and
fit the cot onto them. "Where to, Mrs.?" he asked.

Anna filled in a moment by bending down to wipe Bill's
face and straighten his clothes. It was very hot, the sun
beat down on the tarmac, and great gusts of stale, smoky
air came from the station, where the train from London
had just come in. It was noisy and sticky, and Anna could
not think. Where should she go?

Emmy had woken up, and began to cry in whooping
gasps, arching her back and beating at the air with her
fists. Anna's breasts prickled in reaction to the sound.

"He's hungry, poor mite," the man said. "I have five myself. Brought his bottle, have you?"

"Bottle?" Anna said, "I always feed my babies myself."
She clasped her hands over her empty bosom. She had not

thought of bringing the bottle or the milk. James would be milking the nanny goat now, and wondering when she would be back from her walk. He would be pleased that she had felt well enough to go out. He would think how much better she was getting.

Anna stood on the pavement while Emmy yelled and Billy clutched at her legs and peered through the gateway at the train, and she began to cry herself. Holidaymakers were coming out of the station, children whining after a long, hot journey, fat ladies mopping tactfully at their faces, laden men. Those who noticed the weeping woman steered well clear of her. One small girl said, "Look, Mum, that lady's crying," but her mother yanked harshly at her arm and dragged her away.

The helpful taxi driver raised his eyes to heaven and spread his hands. "Women!" his gesture said, as his mates drove off with their passengers and he had missed the chance of a fare.

Lady Lurie always waited to let the crowds get ahead of her. She could never understand why anyone should queue to get off an aeroplane: she would stay in her seat until the aisle was free for her to walk down at her normal pace. She was the sort of person who always did her Christmas shopping by post in midsummer. The platform was nearly empty when she walked along with her neat suitcase and handbag. She liked to travel light, and all her purchases were being sent. She was sensibly dressed for travelling in a heat wave, in a dark linen dress with her hair hidden under a flowered turban. She enquired after the ticket collector's wife, and he told her about his successes at the South Cornwall Rabbit and Cage Bird Show, and then Lady Lurie came out into the sunshine to find her car.

She did not recognise Anna at first, but would have felt obliged to succour any young woman in evident trouble, specially since Bill had now joined in the chorus of wails. He and Emmy and Anna were oblivious, in their shared misery, to anything around them. Lady Lurie put down her case, went back to the refreshment room, and bought a cup of tea and an ice cream in a cone. She returned briskly to detach Bill's arms from Anna's legs and to pull his face away from her. He had been burrowing his face between her thighs, but was disloyally delighted at the sight of the dripping ice cream and let go at once. Lady Lurie pushed Anna gently onto a bench, and fed her with sips of tea. She said authoritatively to the taxi driver, "Please keep an eye on my friend for me while I telephone," and handed him a pound note. She went to ring River House, but there was no answer from James, or from Tamsin at the cottage. She remembered that Tamsin was to have gone out in a fishing boat, and that Arnold would be fetching the children from school.

Lady Lurie went and opened all the doors and windows of her car, which had been parked for two days in the station yard. She did not want to put the children into it until the air had circulated a little.

"Now, then, Anna," she said, sitting down beside her, "what's all this?"

"I'm going away," Anna muttered, with occasional sobs still catching her breath, "but I forgot Emmy's food. I forgot that she has to have a bottle—"

"All right," Lady Lurie said quickly. "Don't cry again. We'll get her home before it's time to feed her. What about James? Is he here?" and she thought: I wouldn't put it past him, poor fish.

"He doesn't know that I—that we—"

"Come along, then, Anna. Bring Bill to my car. Over here, the yellow one. Now, don't get worked up again; it's so bad for the babies. I know that postnatal depression is very unpleasant, but you must try to control yourself."

Lady Lurie had years of experience, from helping in family planning clinics, charitable organisations for the homeless, shelters for battered wives, and her branch office of the NSPCC, of hysterical young women, and she pushed Anna firmly into the back seat of her car, thanked the taxi driver and set off back to River House.

CHAPTER 10

Tamsin arrived at four o'clock in the morning on the Custom House Quay in Brannell, expecting to meet a gnarled, elderly, rough-voiced fisherman. But Roy Curnow turned out to be a bearded young man who had dropped out from medical school to come home and live a simple life. Simple in some ways it was perhaps, but Tamsin thought it sounded very hard: dawn rising, chancy catches, cutting cold, dangerous seas—and for what? A big income from the few mackerel not already caught in the massive trawls of the Russian, Polish or Scottish ships which came to do what the Cornish fisherman called poaching in the southwestern waters; less chancy shellfish in summer; and most of the profit going toward paying off the initial cost of his boat. He had not much time for spending the money left over, but said that all the pleasure he wanted was to be found in the life itself.

"Where do you sell your fish?" Tamsin asked. "I never see lobsters in Withiel."

"You couldn't afford them, not for the prices we get from foreign buyers. We unload beside a refrigerated lorry, and they are on the Plymouth–Roscoff ferry two hours later. You could be eating one of my lobsters in Maxim's this time tomorrow."

The sun was rising as their boat, with several others, floated smoothly out to sea. Tamsin loved the prospect before her and could bear the smell, of fish and engine oil, but she could not be of any practical help to Roy Curnow and his silent teen-aged brother, and soon began to wish she had brought a book. She could think of a very limited number of questions to ask about the fishing trade, and recorded more of the live sound of a boat at sea than she would ever be able to use. She was not all that keen on the crustaceans, either; the thought of what those steely-blue claws could do to a human body, and of the substances on which they might have fed, disinclined her to think of eating them. At what white bones, she wondered, had they picked?

"Would they feed on human flesh?" she asked.

"You needn't worry," Roy said, surprised. "They can't get out."

"I know, but would they if they could?"

"I suppose so. It's probably very tasty. I say, you aren't feeling sick, are you?"

Later in the morning the pleasure yachtsmen started to appear on the water, dots of colour from their sails sprinkling the blue haze. Tamsin poked a pile of nets into a comfortable shape and reclined in the sun. Very snug . . . it was like rocking in a garden swing. Roy's voice, chatting to his taciturn brother, was comforting, assured and calm. He would have been a good doctor.

"What's that boat putting out now, Stephen? Pass the glasses over a minute."

"That's Simon Wherry's boat. The *Cock's Comb*."

"I thought so. How many on board this time, would you say? Three, four, five . . . He should get a licence for a pleasure boat and make some money from it."

"What do you mean?" Tamsin said.

"Thought you were asleep. Well, if a chap's going to spend his time cruising around with all those gay young things on board, he might as well get a return on it. Must cost him, what with the fuel, and food, and no doubt the gin."

"Where does he take them?"

"Dunno. He's heading south. Could be up the coast, or over to France, or maybe across to the Scillies. Quite a sturdy little craft, the *Cock's Comb*. Must sleep six at least."

"That's never big enough to sail across the Channel!" Tamsin protested.

"Oh yes, you could go round the world in the *Cock's Comb*."

"Just like that? Do you mean he could just sail away?"

"What's to stop him? Oh, you're supposed to give a rough course to the coast guards, and some estimate of when you'll be where, but that's more for your benefit than theirs. I suppose you would need some documents—passport and so on—and enough cash. I've sometimes thought of doing it myself. Set sail for some South Sea island."

"I'm on," Stephen said.

Roy laughed. "Wait till you've got your A Levels. Anyway, look, the *Cock's Comb* is going in again. Simon's girlfriend must be feeling seasick. Come on, Stephen, break out the pasties, put the kettle on. Work for your living, you idle so-and-so."

Tamsin was supposed to be reporting on a typical day at sea, but her presence and the balmy weather relaxed the Curnow brothers, and the afternoon was well on before they were back within hail of Brannell Point and the Grebe.

"Hullo, they've got the harbour launch out," Roy remarked. A smartly painted blue-and-white launch flying a triangular flag was tacking to and fro across the river mouth, and turned to come alongside the Curnows' boat. "Hi, Peter," Roy called. "What's up?"

"Just a routine check. Everything okay?"

"Yeah, sure."

"What have you got aboard, then?"

"Usual catch. Want a cuppa, Pete?"

"As much as my job's worth, boyo. Nah, they are checking everyone that enters the river at the moment on account of those immigrants the other day. They seem to think they might have been aiming at one of the small ports. I can't see it myself. Someone would soon notice all those black faces in a place like Falmouth or Penzance, let alone Brannell. They told us to keep an eye open for drugs too, but of course that's routine."

"Want to come and have a look?"

"Won't bother, Roy, thanks. Not when you've got company," he added, leering mildly at Tamsin. "Who's that, then—Stephen?" he asked, pointing at the pair of trousered legs, visible upside down in the wheelhouse.

"Stephen, naturally. He's relaxing with his girlie mag."

"Get him to save it for me. I'll have to be getting on. I sometimes think they can lip-read from up there on the lookout. Cheers, Roy."

"Cheers, Pete."

"That didn't seem very thorough," Tamsin said once they were out of earshot. "You could have had a whole load of heroin under those baskets."

"Oh, Peter knows me. They all do. After all, I'm in and out practically every day. They might do a spot check now and then just for the record, but they don't bother much, not when they know you."

"I suppose that is reasonable. Still, it must be a loophole."

"I shouldn't think so, not really." Roy throttled down, and his boat slid slowly toward the pier. "They get to know the boats quicker than you'd think. Anyone does that's on the river regularly. You get to notice strange ones; you'd even notice one that was usually tied up. You'd be surprised, some of these boat owners never leave their moorings at all, let alone go out of the river. You notice any visiting craft, and any unusual pattern of behaviour."

"Do you think I should try to get an interview with the coast guards and—who else would it be?"

"All depends. There're several different officials all keeping an eye on the river—from the oyster bailiff to the air—sea rescue people. You'll have your work cut out."

"Oh gosh."

"It's not that bad, actually. They're all very cooperative. Very friendly, maritime people are."

"You certainly have been," Tamsin said warmly. Roy jumped on to the quay and held out his hand for hers. She landed unsteadily beside him.

"Want a job as crew, then?"

"Only if you'll guarantee weather like today's."

"You're a one for indoor comforts, then, are you?"

"Less," Tamsin said, "than I used to be."

In her old life, Tamsin could let days go by without noticing the weather. She had concentrated on interiors—of the house, adorned to suit her exacting husband, and of her personality, in which she made frequent trawls for emotions and reactions, the better to express them in fictional terms.

In Cornwall she was being educated to a less subjective way of life. But she could not imagine denying herself the indefensible benefits of the modern world. She was not yet quite changed from the woman who once said that, if civilisation was doomed, she did not wish to survive it.

As she drew the car, running on the fuel which threatened the sea, and whose burning poisoned the atmosphere, up in front of the cottage, she reflected that the oil company's profits were what paid the rent.

Sir Arnold was teaching his grandchildren to play bridge. They were all sticky, relaxed and not missing her in the least.

Lady Lurie was not back from London yet. She had not lived out of it for long enough to discover that she could get her hair permed or her teeth filled anywhere else.

"I wish she were safely back," Sir Arnold said. "I don't like her to go. Not when there are these letter bombs and parcel bombs going round."

It was the first time Tamsin had ever had occasion to comfort her father, and she felt a brief, sharp pang.

"She's much more likely to be run over in Brannell, Daddy, than hurt in London. Think of the statistics."

"I don't know . . . the modern world."

"Well, they will be aiming at the big nobs, not at Mum," she said comfortingly.

"It doesn't matter who they aim at. Terrorists are dreadfully inefficient. Anyway, what about the ones who don't care whom they kill or mutilate? The lunatics who leave bombs in carrier bags, or send them through the post? Their murders are quite undirected. I don't worry so much about the politicians. They have chosen to stick their necks out. But I wish your mother would not go and risk getting in the way of some kids with a grudge against society."

"She must be nearly back now. Her train should have got in some while ago."

"I shall be glad when she's here."

"You're like a jittery mother hen, Daddy. Is this the man who sat out the Blitz as a firefighter? Is this the man who refused to clear his office for bomb scares? I've often wondered what you would have done if your secretary had been wounded because of your *sangfroid*."

"Nonsense," Sir Arnold muttered, but he looked a little more cheerful, and was soon criticising Tamsin's care of the flower beds with his usual vigour.

"It's too dry," she pleaded. "You can't get a trowel into the ground."

"You must water, then. I'll lend you a hose."

"If it doesn't rain soon, there will be a ban on using them."

"Then you will have to siphon it out of the bath. Soap won't do any harm. It's a nice little garden. Pity to let it spoil."

The previous tenant had been a retired gardener of the Miss Cartwright who had lived at River House. The old man was a rent-protected tenant, and was safe in loathing his new landlords; he hated Anna marginally less than James, but was always rude and disagreeable to them both when they turned in at their own drive. They had told Tamsin that he would lie in wait for them and hiss curses through toothless jaws. His little garden was full of traditional cottage flowers, all of unprecedented size, and he had trained roses around the door and up over the thatched roof. The place looked like an illustration on a chocolate box.

Tamsin was clumsily tying back the pink Albertine roses under her father's direction when Lady Lurie's car drew up at the gate and Anna stumbled out of it. Emmy was asleep, and Bill in a sticky daze. Lady Lurie lifted them out and took firm hold of Anna, turning her steps toward the front door of the cottage.

"Make this girl some tea, Tamsin, will you, with sugar in it? And get her something to eat. I'm sure she's been starving herself. I'll go on up to the house and find James and some milk for the baby, but you'd better take care of these three now. I don't think," she added, whispering, "that Anna's at all well." Anna looked like a person who had given up. She was relaxed and a little vacant. Her clothes were stained with sweat and Bill's ice cream. Pippa came in from her bedroom and, after one hasty glance at Anna, made a surprisingly adult "Keep me out of this" gesture at her mother and bolted. Tamsin brewed tea for three people, and set it out more tidily than usual on the table, to soothe Anna with the forms of conventional life.

The telephone rang when they had been sitting there for several minutes, with Sir Arnold peacefully sipping and reading an ancient copy of the *New Statesman,* and Anna toying with toast and peanut butter. It was Tony Rawe.

"Hi, Tone, how are things?" Tamsin said, relieved by the distraction. She turned her back on the room and watched Ben through the window as he tried to catch a guinea pig which had decided to be free-range. "What? No, I hadn't heard. Well, I must say, it's nice to be sure it wasn't one of those wretched immigrants. What happened? Was he pushed or did he jump? No, I suppose not. Thanks for letting me know." She turned to her father. "It's about that body," she told him. "Good of Tony to let me know. He knew it had been on my mind."

"Don't tell me if you feel you shouldn't," he said, the familiar mark of civil service discretion descending on his face.

"Oh, that's all right. It will all come out when they resume the inquest. Horrid details, actually. Tony didn't tell me much, but apparently the body was dead when it went into the water, as the pathologist said at the inquest. It was so hard to identify because it had been got at by—well, you know. And then the internal gases expanded and it comes to the surface, and by that time there isn't much left to recognise. And there weren't even many clothes left; what the predators didn't get rid of burst off when the internal gas—"

"Tamsin." Sir Arnold looked expressively at Anna. She did not seem to be listening, for her eyes were closed and her head leaning back against the chair; but of course her father was quite right, Tamsin thought. It was only because she had forced herself to come to terms with nausea and horror that she could even think of the corpse at all.

"You're quite right. Thank you. It was just that one thing stayed on, embedded . . . Well, anyway, they found one of those identity bracelets. The sort some men wear around their ankles. The police trace manufacturers, and then they find which shop took deliveries of certain goods, and who bought things—it's amazing what can be traced these days, half across Europe. Interpol found that the bracelet had been made in Germany and sold in Italy, and they think it belonged to a man who was what they call an international anarchist, or something equally unlikely. A German called Karl Fischer. I've never heard of him myself, have you?"

"So that's it," Sir Arnold murmured. "That's where I'd seen—"

"What did you say?" Anna had opened her eyes and jerked herself upright. "What name? Who?"

"It was only about the person who was drowned in the river; nothing for you to worry about. Shall I bring Emmy in to you? My mother should be back any minute."

"Say the name again. Who was he?" Anna's voice was high and urgent.

"It doesn't matter, Anna, my dear. Let it go," Sir Arnold said, and behind her back he put his fingers over his mouth, gesturing Tamsin not to say anything.

"You must tell me. You said it was Karl Fischer, didn't you? I know that's what you said. Tamsin, there, you aren't denying it, I—oh—" She burst into tears and shrieked with laughter at the same time. Bill rushed in, weeping noisily, and clutched at his mother as she stood convulsed by hysterics. Tamsin tried to take him out of the room, but he would not let go, terrified by Anna's behaviour, yet looking to her to save him.

Tamsin knew that she should give Anna an almighty slap across the cheek, but she had never hit anybody, and a lifetime of inhibition held her back. In any case, it surely would not help Billy to watch his mother being clouted.

Lady Lurie, fortunately, was less feeble. She came hurrying into the cottage carrying a bottle full of milk, and took the time to lay it carefully on the table so that the teat would not come into contact with any unsterile surface. She slapped Bill's hand lightly so that he loosened his grip, lifted him up into Tamsin's arms and said crisply, "Take him out of here." As Tamsin was leaving the room she heard the sharp crack of her mother's palm against Anna's cheek, and the uncontrolled noise softened into sobbing. Sir Arnold came out and produced a lollipop from his pocket, which he gave to Bill.

"What was all that about?" Tamsin said. "I know she's ill, but something must have sparked it off. Who is Karl Fischer anyway?"

"I do know, as it happens," her father said absently. He squatted down and began to pull weeds out of the dry soil, and after a moment Bill sat down beside him and dug his hands in and out of the earth. "Karl Fischer was active in the student movements all over Europe a few years ago. He was sent to prison in France after a riot at the Sorbonne, but he must have come out some time ago. I suppose he's been lying low since then."

"Was he over here?" Tamsin asked curiously. Sir Arnold had rarely talked about his work at home, but she knew that in his last years at the Home Office he had been in the branch concerned with the deportation of agitators, and there had been one occasion when his name was mentioned at question time in the House of Commons as having taken part in the persecution of an anarchist leader. Fortunately for Tamsin's own relationship with her college friends, that particular victim of bureaucratic bullies was shortly to be convicted of murdering the prostitute on whose earnings he had been living, because she had decided to transfer her services to another ponce.

"Karl Fischer was here for several years," Sir Arnold

said. "He was reading something like sociology or politics, and came in on a student's visa. He kept his head down for some time, and he had a good mind, his teachers said; a bit ineffectual perhaps. Anyway, he started to stir up trouble, and eventually left only just in time. We were about to apply for a deportation order."

"Why do you remember the case so well?"

"There were certain complications. He'd left some relations behind in this country. You know how difficult these things can be. Ah, there's your mother. How is she, Jean?"

"I have telephoned for an ambulance," Lady Lurie said.

"But Mum—"

"It's no good, Tamsin. I had a word with James, and he's coming as soon as he has got rid of the busload of visitors in the gallery. Anna refuses to see her general practitioner, whom she very much dislikes. He was not at all sympathetic to natural childbirth when Emmy was born, he would not let James stay in the room, and there was rather an unpleasant scene. But Anna obviously needs proper care; she's quite ill. I have seen enough of this sort of thing to know. I had a word with our own doctor in Brannell, and he agreed to take her as a private patient for the time being, and said I should have her admitted at once."

"That seems a little bit drastic. Surely there isn't all that much wrong with her?"

"In any normal household you might be right. But it's too much for you, Tamsin; the responsibility isn't fair to you, and you know what James is like. I can't find that there is anyone else to help. Anna is an orphan, James tells me, and has no relations. It will be just as well for her to be away from the children for a while too; you never know what might happen. Better for her and them."

"But Anna would never lift a finger against the children," Tamsin said.

"You never know what women who are having a bad postnatal depression will do. No, my dear, my doctor quite agrees with me. James will be able to cope with Billy and Emmy if Anna's being well looked after."

Anna made no protest as she was led into the ambulance.

James went with her, holding himself stiffly as though he were more afraid than she. Tamsin just hoped he would be able to control himself until Anna was well sedated.

CHAPTER 11

The national press reported the body in the River Brann in minimal detail. Even to the local weekly, the *Withiel Times and Scrutineer,* it was of less importance than the council's intention to raise car-parking charges, and suspicions of sexual licence at the comprehensive school.

The identification of the body from the estuary was announced on the centre page.

LOCAL BOY FINDS INTERNATIONAL BODY

Mr. Lumb, the Withiel coroner, sitting this week at the resumed inquest on the body found last month at Longwood Creek, was told by Inspector Gemmell that the corpse carried identification which indicated it to be that of Karl Fischer, alias the Goldfish, also known as Peter Hurst, and Charles or Pierre Durand. Evidence was given by the Hydrographic Officer of the Navy, stationed at RN Air Station Brannell, to the effect that a body which entered the water some miles out to sea might have been beached at the head of Longwood Creek. There was an exceptionally high tide during that week. There is so far no evidence to show that Fischer, who was a prohibited immigrant, entered the United Kingdom at any port or airport. The death is being treated as a case of foul play, and Interpol have been consulted. The pathologist, Dr. Michael Woodforde, has not been able to state the cause of death, though it is not thought to have been drowning. Identification of the remains was made by means of an identity bracelet. The hands and feet had suffered extensive mutilation after prolonged immersion, and it was not possible to take fingerprints.

Fischer is not known to have consulted a dentist using any of the above names. Inspector Gemmell stated that the investigation was proceeding, and the inquest was adjourned.

The young man from the Public Health Department who had been to Grebe never read the *Withiel Times and Scrutineer*, being in a branch of local government which was rarely criticised or even reported.

Councillor Mrs. Lumb read the local paper from cover to cover, in the hope of detecting the forbidden use of private premises for commercial purposes by recognising the same telephone number in the classified advertisements too often, or in the expectation of finding that some acquaintance's activities, or, better still, her own, were reported in suitable detail. She prided herself on knowing every last detail of what went on in her district.

She was a slow thinker, but a thorough one, and rarely spoke or acted on impulse. She meditated for a while about the best thing to do. Her husband, after all, who never told her the tiniest hint of a secret connected with his work, had been the very coroner whose words were now printed beside the photograph, an official full-face and profile "mug shot" of Karl Fischer. Eventually she decided that she was a good citizen before she was a well-connected one. She went to stand at the desk in the police station, just like any obscure little housewife reporting the loss of a purse.

A team of officers, with their substructure of clerks and typists, had been assigned to the problem of the body when it was first found, but even then there seemed no special reason for supposing that it had any particular connection with the area. The erratic action of the ocean currents in this part of the western approaches was well known, and flotsam and jetsam had been observed to turn up on the shores of the River Brann which must have entered the water far out to sea. Some oceanographers from the University of Buriton had published a study of this subject two years before, and concluded that the configuration of the sea floor, the action of the prevailing southwest winds, and the fact that the Brann estuary faces into them, combined to ensure that 61 percent more floating objects would eventually be deposited on the banks of the Brann than on other local landfalls. The admission of a natural cause for the appearance of so many foreign artefacts in this part of Cornwall had come as a relief to the archaeologists who studied it. They had previously been forced to distressingly implausible explanations for their random finds.

Inspector Gemmell and his Superintendent had therefore felt, one relieved, and the other disappointed, that there was not much they themselves could do about the body which was later shown to be that of Karl Fischer. While maintaining the investigation locally to a certain extent, they had handed copies of their files over to Scotland Yard and to the International Police.

When Mrs. Lumb arrived at the police station, neither of the two men was available. Gemmell was working on a complicated fraud enquiry about a trade in pension books, and Superintendent Polglaze was trying to coordinate the proofs of evidence for the prosecution of a man accused of living with his family on the proceeds of a robbery in the Home Counties. This family had bought a large farmhouse inland from Withiel and lived an apparently blameless life, with children at the village school and regular appearances at local festivities. They were very popular in the neighbourhood because they always paid for everything in ready cash. The premises had already been searched twice; the second time the police had gone to the length of having the kitchen range levered up from its base. No cache of pound notes had been found under it. This week the Superintendent had come across an article by a local historian about domestic economy in the preindustrial period, and learnt that before the invention of refrigerators perishable food used to be kept cool in cavities in the sides of well shafts. Superintendent Polglaze was planning a lightning swoop for the early hours of the next morning.

Mrs. Lumb had to tell her story first to a constable and then to a sergeant. But eventually she was able to inform the men in charge of the investigation that she had seen and spoken to a man whose appearance matched the photograph of Karl Fischer, and that had been at Grebe, less than three weeks before.

CHAPTER 12

Sir Arnold Lurie, who had reached the top in a service noted for caution, was in the habit of checking his facts before acting on them.

He rang his club to book a bedroom, and on Wednesday morning was waiting on Truro Station for the train, equipped for London in pinstripes and bowler hat, carrying his old briefcase with the crown on it and his rolled umbrella. He read a biography of the Duke of Wellington on the train, and was easily able to keep his disciplined, compartmented mind from considering the problem which was taking him to London until he had gathered some more data.

"Sir Arnold, sir, it's good to see you." The doorman at the Department was touchingly pleased when Sir Arnold walked in, and hurried from his cubbyhole to shake hands. "We miss you, sir, we do indeed. I'll never forget those nights we spent on the roof during the war, sir, I was thinking of it only this week. You were there, and Mr. Banting that's gone now, poor gentleman, and his lordship as is now. Do you remember the incendiary you put out in a bucket? And the time we saw the flames over on the theatre roof . . . ?"

He babbled on. It was good of the old chap to be so affectionate, but Arnold had heard his sentimental reminiscences many times before. He did not remember with any pleasure himself the days of bombing raids on London. Fire watching had been cold, wet and uncomfortable, and above all boring, and he marvelled, not for the first time, at the human instinct to glorify the unpleasant past.

"Ah well, those were the days," the old man wound up.

"Those were the days. Who shall I let know you're here, sir? Mr. Illingworth is in the building, I know."

"No, don't bother, thanks, McKie. I want to go down to the archives. I'll find my own way."

Arnold Lurie was always impressed by these banks and rows of files; it was as though every hair on the heads of the people who came into contact with this section of the Ministry had been listed for posterity. He walked between the stacks. There was the file on the Chakrabongse case; sad one, that, and he was never sure that they had reached the right conclusion. And Emmanuel Dessai—what a troublesome case that had been, only resolved in the end by the Court of Appeal. As Sir Arnold had always reminded his staff, they were dealing with people, not with reference numbers or with names on a grey cardboard file. Administrators must enforce the laws enacted by Parliament, but must be careful not to forget that they were human beings.

Fanjieh, Feinstein, Fezaqh. He drew out the file on Karl Fischer and took it over to a table under one of the thick glass panels let into the pavement. The daylight was periodically obscured as pedestrians walked above him.

The file was bulging with copies of letters, appeals and court proceedings. Several of the letters were carbons of those which Arnold Lurie had signed himself; this had been a troublesome case.

Karl Fischer was a typical waif, a piece of human driftwood cast up by Europe's storms. He was born in 1945 to a girl released from a concentration camp, and an unknown father. His mother did not survive his birth, and he was brought up in an orphanage.

By the time he was fifteen, he had decided to become the next generation's Karl Marx, or even its Lenin. He studied politics and law at the University of Munich, and then went to Ferraby, in the English Midlands, as a postgraduate. Nobody denied that he was clever; that was part of the trouble.

He might well have had short-lived plans to inspire a new world from the British Museum Reading Room. But he had soon joined, and then found himself organising, the militant students' movement, and saw a quicker road to achievement than reading and writing. He accepted the premise that you can't make an omelette without breaking eggs, and began to preach that only violence would produce change. He took part in strikes, marches and sit-ins, and spent a good deal of his time in visiting other universities, in Britain and Europe, to carry on the message.

In 1970, Fischer had married another foreign student, Anna Grete Cohen. Her papers were in a separate file, and Sir Arnold went to fetch it from the shelves. It was even thicker than Fischer's. Arnold Lurie, who had come to London specially to reread it, found himself hesitating to turn the cover back. He went upstairs and asked the porter to have him brought some coffee, and waited until his successor's secretary brought it down, in the porcelain cup and saucer he had used for a quarter of a century, placed on a tray cloth and flanked with identical biscuits.

Anna Cohen's parents had worked as doctors in what had been India, later became East Pakistan, and eventually Bangladesh. Mrs. Cohen had been born Harriet Selwood, and her daughter Anna was the third generation of her missionary family, originally from Middlesbrough, to be born in the family house in Nepal. Anna, though born on this visit home to Katmandu, was a Pakistani citizen, since her parents were domiciled in that country. In fact, after the war her father, Wilhelm Cohen, who had been a refugee from Hitler's Germany, resumed his own German nationality. Anna was sent to a boarding school run by a Low Church charity in the north of England, and then went to Ferraby to study the history of art. In 1968 she met Karl Fischer, and married him when she became pregnant—in order, as was perfectly clear at the time, to retain the right to stay in the United Kingdom. She was too unwell to continue with the course of education for which she had been granted her own residence permit.

When the child, Theodore, was born, Karl Fischer was already in the hands of the French police. Anna's permission to stay in the country was renewed on compassionate grounds because the child needed regular medical treatment. Fischer received a prison sentence in France and could not contribute to his support. In 1972 Theodore died.

What made the case so difficult, and caused Sir Arnold Lurie much sympathetic worry, was that, while she had been living in Ferraby, Anna Fischer's own family had disappeared.

Her brother, Peter Cohen, who had been studying medicine in London, flew back to Pakistan when the troubles began there in 1971. Sheikh Mujibor Rahman had demanded a better deal for East Pakistan from President Yahya Khan, who replied by declaring martial law. Peter Cohen said he would be back in time to start the next term at London University; he promised his sister not to be gone for long, but said he felt he had to fight for freedom.

During the last week of March, the army of West Pakistan took control of the major cities of East Pakistan, and soon after that news filtered out of the country about the formation of a group of freedom fighters calling themselves the Mukti Bahini. News trickled sparsely out of the beleaguered country, and the rest of the world knew little more than that the armies of the West had inflicted massacres on the "East," and many victims described as "intellectuals" had perished.

Neither Peter Cohen, nor his parents, the two doctors, were ever heard of again. Efforts were made to trace them, on Anna Fischer's behalf, since the allegedly heartless department for which Arnold Lurie worked actually maintained a large welfare branch. But even after the state of Bangladesh had been recognised by the government of India, and eventual peace came to a country whose economy was in ruins, many people, of all classes, remained untraced.

So there was no help to come to Anna Fischer from her home.

Arnold Lurie looked at the photograph pinned inside the cover of the file; she had changed since it was taken. It was understandable that his memory had been jogged, not by meeting the older Anna, but by seeing Ivory Judd's portrait of her as a student. The photograph showed a gentle-faced

girl with faintly slanted cheekbones and eyes; not clever,
not dynamic, but a girl born to be a good mother and a lov-
ing wife, not fitted to be caught up in political upheavals.
Even at the time, he had felt that the regulations he was
obliged to administer were inhuman.

There had been a row, rare in Arnold Lurie's disciplined
life, with Elkins. He hated to think how the Department
would be run if careerists like that brash young man
reached the top.

"I see the child has died," Elkins had remarked, leafing
through the file on Fischer and inserting the latest report.
"It turned out to be a congenital abnormality of the blood
in the end—though he was run over, actually. Funny, I always suspected she was making the whole thing up to get
her residence permit extended. We're too generous with
the Health Service; it's folly to be excessively compassionate, I always think. Ah well, we can deport the girl
now, I suppose."

"Let me see," Sir Arnold Lurie said in a dangerously
quiet voice. The report was brief, a supplement to earlier
accounts of the treatment Theodore Fischer had been receiving at Ferraby General Hospital. He was not quite two
years old when he died. Arnold read it slowly, and then
said, "You should not refer to a child's death in that manner, Elkins."

"Oh, sir—a fatherless two-year-old with a feckless
mother? What sort of a life would he have had?"

"That is not the way to measure the value of a human
life."

"I'm sorry, sir, but I think that's dangerous senti-
mentality. Of course I wouldn't dream of saying we should
actually get rid of the useless members of society, though
I'm all in favour of a judicious spot of euthanasia—voluntary, that is. But once the kid is dead anyway, one might as
well admit relief. I wouldn't say so in front of the mother,
naturally."

"How old are you, Elkins?"

"I am twenty-eight, sir."

"Married?"

"No, sir, not yet."

"Well," Arnold shouted, "I hope for every wretched girl's sake that you never will be. And I hope you never get your hands on any innocent child. I've never heard such a display of callous, heartless inhumanity. You should work in a department where you have no dealings with people, and no control over their lives. Good morning to you."

Elkins left the room looking astonished, and Arnold heard the whispering outside his door. He had never lost his temper at the office before. There was probably a gaggle of giggling typists listening out there. He heard his own secretary's voice above the rest.

"Never you mind, Mr. Elkins. I daresay he's worried about something just at present. Perhaps his daughter is having another baby. It takes some grandfathers like that."

"Sympathetic morning sickness, I suppose," Elkins said loudly. "Will he go in for *couvade* as well?"

Sir Arnold had thought carefully, and then written to the right man recommending that Elkins be advised to apply for a transfer from the Home Office.

Anna Fischer, as a foreign national married to another foreign national, without the benefit of British parents or grandparents, no longer had either legal or compassionate grounds to be granted an extension of her permit to stay in the United Kingdom. At the end of 1973 she was escorted onto a ferry taking day trippers to Calais and advised not to return, as she would not be permitted to enter the country again.

Arnold Lurie had spent forty years making decisions, and even now he was retired, it should have come easily to him. He knew, as he sat at the little table in the basement of his old office, what he should do. It was almost unprecedented for him to feel as indecisive as he did at this moment. His professional life had not nurtured his initiative or independence. When it came to the crunch, there had always been a rule book—with rules that could be bent, perhaps, or applied in a civilised British way; but on paper he could always find a theoretical solution; and, if by any chance the rules did not provide for a particular problem, there were always his masters to appeal to, the elected decision-makers. The buck did not often stop at Arnold Lurie's desk.

Today he had no Minister upstairs to answer his question.

Arnold did not want to tell the authorities what he knew about Anna Buxton; and, if he did not do so, it was unlikely that anyone else would be in a position to destroy the life she had created for herself and her family.

Arnold liked Anna; he had bought Ivory Judd's painting of her not only because of the twinge of recognition he had experienced when he saw it, but also because it showed a serene, sympathetic creature designed by nature to soothe and cheer and cherish. Arnold's own wife and daughter were the kind of women he loved: clever and able, at home in the modern world, but somewhere Arnold had a buried hankering for the old-fashioned kind of feminine woman.

He thought about the late Karl Fischer, this sweet girl's first husband. He had started out as a typically rootless iconoclast. He had a certain gift of the gab, and did quite well on soapboxes, but probably attracted his followers because he invited them to do with him what they wanted, in any case, to do even without him. He released their inhibitions about throwing things and shouting and breaking what they had been brought up to cherish. None of the authorities with whom he had come into conflict expected him to be capable of much greater harm than that, though there were hints that he had joined a commune of even less governed souls than himself. The report from the Paris police at the back of his file merely said that he had been convicted of assaulting a policeman, which was a matter taken seriously by French courts. But the riot in which he had been taking part was, on the whole, a milk-and-water affair compared with the fighting on the barricades in 1968. However, it was of course likely that Karl Fischer would have learnt a good deal about criminality while he was in prison.

Sir Arnold agreed with the various estimates of his personality made by the authorities through whose hands Fischer had been during the time that this file was being compiled: he would be tiresome rather than dangerous;

and had been, apparently, sufficiently tiresome for someone to kill him—or at least chuck his dead body unceremoniously into the sea.

Arnold Lurie usually had a faint admiration for those who put themselves in danger for the sake of a principle, no matter how perverse that principle might be. But he was not sorry that Karl Fischer was dead. He had not been worthless. But he had been worth much less than Anna.

Sir Arnold thought of Anna as he had so recently seen her, weeping and then dazed. He felt sure that her collapse had been caused by her estimable feminine instincts being assailed by the news of Fischer's death.

He wished his duty was not so inescapably plain.

CHAPTER 13

"Another piece of inside information?" Tamsin said to
Tony Rawe. "Where do you get these titbits, anyway?" She
was beginning to wonder whether to believe everything he
told her, always in strictest confidence, and not always
confirmed later.

"Small-town life, my love. You know Ferdy, don't you,
that lived with me? You did meet him once. Well, as it happens, Ferdy's brother is straight; he's a real butch type,
works down in the docks and plays soccer on Saturdays. So
this guy—he's called Tim, friend of Ferdy's—Tim's girlfriend is a typist at the police station. She's been vetted and
all that, pure as the driven snow, signed the Official Secrets
Act, you know the scene. So she crosses her little pinkies
when she's promising not to tell, because of course she has
to tell Tim everything. She's that sort of girl. Anyway, Tim
doesn't count; as far as she's concerned, they are as near
one flesh as makes no difference, though I don't have the
impression he thinks so. Well, he hasn't sworn anything,
has he? And if he tells Ferdy and Ferdy tells me that Dawn
typed out a memo saying that the body you found in the
water wasn't Karl Fischer's after all, then I might as well
tell you. Don't you agree?"

"Do they know whose it was?"

"They say it was Simon Wherry's."

Tamsin put the telephone receiver down. She was suddenly feeling very peculiar. She dashed into the bathroom
and was violently sick. It was bad enough to find a decomposed body which was later identified as being that of a
strange foreigner. But to remember Simon Wherry, and

think of him as she had seen that thing in the mud—she had to go and vomit again.

The death must have been an accident. But if he had simply fallen into the river the body would have been found before it became so dreadfully mutilated. If Simon had met with a fatal accident out at sea, and fallen into the water, how had the *Cock's Comb* returned to her mooring, where she was now prettily floating? Could he have fallen from a friend's boat? James and Anna owned a little motor launch, and many other people in the neighbourhood had boats. But anybody from whose boat Simon fell would have both noticed and reported it.

In any case, Tamsin thought, she had seen the *Cock's Comb* sailing in and out of the estuary many times since the estimated date of death.

Tamsin realised that Simon Wherry must have been murdered.

Murder was quite outside her frame of reference; she shared with the majority of people a complete inexperience of violence. What's more, she had never followed newspaper reports of crimes, or found murder fiction in the least bit plausible. She had always lived in an environment where excesses were verbal. Her assessments of human relationships could envisage nothing more extreme than a husband's palm raised to slap, or a wife's to throw. She did not believe in guns or daggers, arsenic or dynamite, though recently there had been moments when Tamsin could have wished Clarissa dead, if not Alex.

But she did not wish even Clarissa dead anymore. By appreciating what Alex had rejected, Simon had enabled Tamsin to retrieve a necessary self-esteem. Now that he was dead, she could forgive him for turning her out of Grebe. Before, she might have seemed to have a motive to wish some harm to Simon herself.

Tamsin knew someone whose motive was more real than hers. But since she had lived by, and written about, the paramount importance of human relationships, could she now destroy the friendship she had made with the Buxtons, just because it seemed expedient to do so? She really did not feel that she could go to the police and say that she knew who had the best motive for disposing of Simon Wherry; it would not be she who told them about James's Paradise Lost, nor that it was now perhaps Regained.

Tamsin started to make tea for Pippa and Ben. Ben had recently got into the nasty habit of asking her to guess what Daddy and Clarissa would be having to eat—ice cream? steak? or, treat of all treats, dinner in a Chinese restaurant? Alex, out of carelessness or malice, had fed the children, when he took them out on Sunday, with a lavishness which would have been more suitable for his transatlantic visitors. Irritated by herself for giving in to the defensive impulse, Tamsin began to prepare a much better meal than the children needed. They should have had salad again, which was the only appropriate food for this weather. But tonight they were getting roast chicken with all the trimmings, and strawberry fool.

She put a sliver of lemon peel into the fowl's carcase. Tomorrow, she thought, they would take baskets to the farm where they could pick their own soft fruit. Pippa needed new sandals. Ben must get a present to take to his friend's birthday party. She must ring to see whether her father was back from London. She must ask Tony whether he could use an interview with a woman who collected old paperback Westerns. She must read the small print of the local paper to see what boats were for sale secondhand. Tamsin pushed that idea aside; it was too close to the subject she was trying to avoid thinking about.

Inspector Gemmell and his Sergeant arrived at the cottage while Tamsin was whipping the cream for the pudding. They walked up the garden path in their shirtsleeves, and one of them picked a leaf from the lemon verbena and rubbed it under his nose. She thought they were salesmen, or perhaps tourists wanting cream teas, and she went out into the blazing light to send them away.

They introduced themselves, and she invited them to sit in the garden. "Such a pity everything is dying in this drought," she said nervously. The patch of grass they were sitting on was brown, and the roses, which had been a silken pink the week before, had wilted into faded, colourless lumps on the stalk. "Would you like a cold drink? Lemonade? Beer?"

They seemed pleased, and she went in and put glasses and ice cubes and a jug of fruit juice on a tray, slowly because she wanted to decide what to say. But she could not concentrate her mind; it kept sliding off into irrelevancies. She picked some mint and let it float on the lemonade.

"Thank you, madam," the older man said. That was the Sergeant; he had said his name, but in her confusion she had forgotten it.

"Very welcome indeed," Inspector Gemmell agreed. "Mr. Buxton didn't offer us anything, and it's scorching today. We're not allowed to ask, you know."

"You've been up to the house already?"

"Yes, we've had a word with Mr. Buxton. But that won't surprise you, Mrs. Oriel. Is that right—Mrs. Tamsin Jane Oriel?"

"Yes, that's right."

The Sergeant wrote it down, but then laid the pad and pen on the ground beside him.

"Just an informal call, madam. We might ask you to come down to the station and make a statement later—to sign, you know. I just thought we would have a little chat first."

"I . . . what about?"

Inspector Gemmell raised his eyebrows. Tamsin reminded herself that she was not supposed to know that the body was really Simon's. That typist would get into trouble if she let on that . . . She said, "I have heard that you've identified the body as Simon Wherry's."

"Oh? Where did you hear that?"

"On the grapevine. You know how it is. So I thought you might come round to ask some questions."

"The grapevine?"

"You don't expect a journalist to reveal her sources, do you? As I expect you know, I work for Radio Withiel." A scenario flashed through her mind, of questions, prosecution, a martyrdom in prison because of her professional in-

tegrity. But the Inspector only said, "Never can keep secrets in a place like Withiel. So you know who we think the
body was. What have you got to tell us?"

"Nothing really. But I wish you would tell me how you
can be sure. Am I allowed to ask that?"

"Why not?" He winked at his subordinate, and Tamsin
thought: It's silly to try chatting up this man; he's smarter
than I am. "It isn't difficult to identify a body if you know
what you are looking for, Mrs. Oriel. His teeth were on record with his dentist, so once we knew which dentist to ask,
it was no problem. Very careful of his teeth, was Mr.
Wherry."

"How did he die? Was he drowned?"

"We are treating the case as one of foul play, madam."

"I . . . I don't know what to say. What do you want me
to tell you?" She sounded nervous, and the two men exchanged glances. She could see that they inferred she had
something to tell them. "I haven't anything to tell you," she
said. "I hardly knew him. I only moved here in the spring."

"When did you last see Mr. Wherry, madam?"

"Umm . . . let me think. Well, I saw him on the *Cock's
Comb,* or at least I thought I did, not long ago. Though
now I wonder . . . It was the day I went out in Roy Curnow's fishing boat. You can ask them, Roy and his brother,
they saw the *Cock's Comb* too. We talked about it."

"Did you actually see a man you thought was Simon? Or
just his boat?"

"I thought I saw him. We weren't very close. But I did
wave to him."

"What was he wearing? What did he look like? Can you
remember?"

"The usual things people do wear—jeans, one of those
denim caps with a peak, sunglasses. Nothing special."

"In fact, as he had a beard, you saw little of the man's
features. I assume the man you saw had a beard?"

"Yes, of course. You know that Simon did."

"Could it have been someone other than Mr. Wherry?"

"It's possible. In fact, I suppose it must have been,
though it never occurred to me at the time."

"Never occurred to anyone else, either," the Sergeant said. He flicked through the pages of his notebook. "Coast guards, Harbour Master, Customs man—the lot of them thought they saw him on several occasions. They were so used to seeing him go out in his boat."

"They say that one perceives what one expects to see," Tamsin said.

"Exactly so, Mrs. Oriel. Now, let's see. You have a good view of the river from here. You must have been able to watch Mr. Wherry quite often."

"Yes, I thought I did. But it might have been someone dressed like him. What do all those friends he had staying at Grebe say?"

"They have all gone, Mrs. Oriel. The place is deserted," Gemmell told her. "How well did you know him, madam?"

She thought: How well did I know him? Perfectly, at first sight, and then progressively less well, until she had not known him at all. They'd recognised one another, she thought, but found that they were strangers after all.

They had met at one of Anna's private-view parties, shortly after Tamsin moved to the cottage and shortly before Emmy was born; Anna gliding slowly about the room in a dress like an awning; Tamsin thought of the hackneyed simile which likens pregnant women to sailing ships, and rejected it, meaning to think of a better one when she had time; James darted around like a tug, directing Anna to buyers and dealers and newly arrived visitors. There were watercolours of the estuary on the walls, sweeps of pale colours which merged into each other. Aluminium sculptures of birds and small rodents were arranged on glass shelves. James had already sold a coffee table made from holly wood.

Tamsin was feeling her way, uncertain what the language would be. She had dressed anonymously, not wanting to commit herself to a personality yet. She did not want to be Tamsin Oriel, the writer, or Mrs. A. D. W. Oriel, wife of the brilliant . . . daughter of the distinguished . . . For the time being she was a silent, unobtrusive observer.

The room was dominated by the painter's cousins, over

for the day from Devonshire; they had come to see whether anyone would pay good money for Rob's daubs and exclaimed loudly when three purchasers did. Tamsin watched them carefully, to get the details right in her notebook later: father, rust-red and glistening; mother, sharp of face, breasts, hipbones and voice; their pigeon pair of children, firmly bulging out of their clothes. The whole family wore knitted nylon sports shirts which outlined their various protuberances—on the man, where he must once have had muscles; on his wife, where she was encased in rigid nylon. The boy had modelled his behaviour on the gangsters in movies. The girl giggled and twitched her hips, and a balloon of flesh showed through the gap between her shirt and her short skirt.

"Imagine them as the Swiss Family Robinson," a voice murmured above Tamsin's left ear. She turned to see Simon Wherry, his whole appearance a contrast to that of the man he was watching. He was tall, thin, clean and casual, a contrast also to Alex, who would at this time be adjusting the fit of his plum-coloured velvet jacket, and letting Clarissa tie his evening bow.

Tamsin spent the evening playing an almost forgotten game; putting forward conversational pawns and taking his with swift verbal pounces; meeting his eyes with hers, conversing in the allusive manner of two people who understand one another. She had thought it was the start of . . . well, she did not want to be precise about what their relationship might lead to.

What had they had together? Two dinners in Withiel restaurants; two afternoons indoors at the cottage, with an eye on the clock to be ready for the children's return from school; a brief sail in the *Cock's Comb*, which was spoiled for Tamsin by a bitter wind and a stink of fuel; a lot of chat. They had laughed, quite kindly, about James's primitive ambitions.

"He should have been born a hundred years later," Tamsin said. "I see him as the pioneer of the future on an earth-type planet."

"I doubt if he'd be dynamic enough for that."

"You may be right. And it wouldn't be much fun for Anna. Women pioneers had to do most of the dirty work. And there wouldn't be anyone to paint or buy watercolours of the estuary, or aluminium voles."

"No, the middlewoman would be out there hoeing with the rest of them."

"Or perhaps—" Tamsin could not resist embroidering the idea, though she felt lowered by her own disloyalty, "James would build her a loom and she'd weave their tunics."

There had been something about Simon which brought out the worst side of her, the cattiness and spite, the louche and randy self which was usually concealed by aloofness. The very first time she saw him, at Anna's gallery, her mind had rushed to bed.

Inspector Gemmell and his Sergeant were waiting to hear how well she had known Simon.

She said calmly, "I knew him moderately well, for a very little while. We saw one another a few times in the spring, but since then hardly at all."

"When was the last occasion on which you saw him to talk to?"

"I went to Grebe with James Buxton in early May, but hardly spoke to him then. He was busy with his other visitors."

"And before that?"

Tamsin remembered the day in detail. Balmy weather, the beginning of the long, hot summer, but then, without foresight, just a day of rare perfection, not to be wasted. They found a hollow in the woods, soft mossy ground under the fresh green of the stunted oaks. A faint smell of mud and sea floated up from the estuary, and of ferns and flowers from the riverbank. Birds, boats and, when she and Simon were still, a pair of grey squirrels. She had said, "I could send the children to my parents for the night."

"Not on, I'm afraid. I'm off on the evening tide."

"Oh, Simon. Must you?"

"Yup. I've got an appointment."

"Why don't I come along too?"

He pushed her away and sat up, his mood already detached from her. "No, I've got things to do. Maybe I'll see you when I'm back. Sometime next week."

But he hadn't seen her when he was back. She had watched the *Cock's Comb* come in, and Simon and his party of merrymakers row ashore in his dinghy. Others had come down to the jetty to welcome them; and Tamsin had sat at her window, seeing the girls and men on the other side of the water, and felt her face grow tight with envy that she was not free to sail and drink and dance, but was stuck alone with the children doing chores like sewing up the crotch of Ben's trousers, and finding a ball of string and six jam jars for Pippa's school project. During the days that followed she had concluded that she was doomed to be supplanted by tall, thin girls with long red hair who were ten years younger than she was. Simon had whizzed past her in Withiel, driving his dark-green car, with a carbon copy of Clarissa at his side.

Tamsin said to the waiting policemen, "It must have been in the second half of April, just after the children went back to school. I was going for a walk in the woods over there, and met Simon Wherry. He said he was setting off in the *Cock's Comb* that evening."

The Inspector and the Sergeant heaved themselves out of the deck chairs.

"We heard that you had dinner out with Mr. Wherry more than once," Gemmell said, as he walked towards the gate, with Tamsin like a polite hostess at his side. "Would you have known him well enough to have any guesses who might have wished him dead?"

"I knew very little about Mr. Wherry's life," she said coldly. "I don't even know how he earned his living, or who his friends were—apart from seeing him on his boat with lots of them. There isn't much more I can tell you."

The children came round the corner and started to run when they saw Tamsin at the gate. She opened her arms to Ben, a maternal woman committed to domesticity, and she stood with her hands in her children's as the policemen drove away.

CHAPTER 14

The nurses and doctors kept Anna very heavily sedated at first. She lay in bed inertly, without thought. After a while she came to realise that simply to admit to herself that at this time she could not cope was helping her to recover, and cope again. To have decisions taken out of her hands was enough, for the moment; to be able to stop worrying was medicine itself.

It was not as though she had been uneasy about Karl ever since she first came to Cornwall. It was never logical to fear that he would turn up, after all, and during the last year or so she had been reminded of him less and less often, and had managed to banish his pursuing image, as she had banished her fears of death or mutilation for the children.

The sight of Karl had been all the greater shock. She saw him driving through the main street of Withiel and was shattered by terror and dismay.

The day had started as a happy one; she had walked into town, that early summer morning, to deliver Billy to his nursery school, and the trivial nature of her preoccupations had engendered an unthinking contentment. She had bought what she needed: some unrefined sugar, a small sack of vegetable protein, some ginseng tablets, a soothing cream for the children's skin made without cruelty to animals. She had drawn some money from the bank, a respectable citizen with her own cheque-book and a sizeable credit balance; she was on her way home to her virtuous husband and her healthy babies.

And there had been Karl Fischer, not twenty metres away, as large, hairy, virile and self-confident as ever.

Anna bolted behind somebody's front hedge, and cowered, shivering, behind the dusty privet leaves as the van, with its dented wing and broken mirror, drove by.

He had not seen her.

Or had he seen her? You could not tell with Karl. He had not given any sign of seeing her.

Perhaps he wouldn't care if he had recognised Anna. She had always told herself that he would hardly have noticed that she was gone. He would have been perfectly all right without her. And without the baby? That was a question to avoid.

What could Karl have been doing in Withiel? She could not imagine that he was, like most of the people in Cornwall in the summer, just on holiday. He wasn't the type of person who had holidays. He wasn't the type of person who came to Cornwall. She would not have thought that he had ever heard of it.

For a day or so, Anna hoped, against reason, that she had seen Karl Fischer by coincidence. But, then, what about the face she'd seen, in the evening, at her window? Reason told her she had imagined it, but terror was not susceptible to such arguments. Karl was looking for Anna, and for what Anna had taken away from him.

She could not now regret his death.

Anna lay in hospital recuperating from fear. She swallowed the drugs she was given, ate meat, white bread, and adulterated substances of all kinds. She watched television programmes with enjoyment and listened to Palm Court music. She accepted compliments on her family, whose photographs stood on her table, and agreed with her neighbour that James was a "dish."

And all the time she was thinking back to a period she had only veiled, not obliterated, in her memory.

It was years ago now, and she could be calm about it. At first, when it was all fresh in her mind, especially after Billy was born, she had hardly been able to forgive herself for her acquiescence in Karl's plans. How could she have sat listening to discussions of explosions, death, riots and violence? She had even contributed ideas, welcomed plans to harm the society which had battered her. She had been unbalanced, of course, after Theodore died, and after her two years of living death.

Anna had lived in the bed-sitting-room into which she and Karl had moved when they married. They covered the cracks in the walls with posters, and used the bed, which took up most of the room, both as a table and a sofa. The other families living in the house were immigrants, and Anna would have liked to make friends with them. She had grown up in a country where some women lived in huts and covered their faces from the world, and she understood their modesty. Nor did she flinch, as Karl did, when the husbands hit and shouted at their wives. That was just the way things were; since early childhood, Anna had accepted that the neighbours of her own emancipated family included some of the most oppressed humans alive.

But the other women did not understand the dialects Anna spoke, and evidently feared her as much as any of the other immodest females they saw through their draperies, as they shuffled out into the world to buy food, with silent gestures, before retreating to their safe cages.

It would have been nice to be able to converse with her neighbours after Karl had gone. At first friends from the university came to visit. Ivory Judd would arrive with cheering-up presents like sesame seeds or incense sticks; the boys, who were more Karl's friends than Anna's, paid dutiful calls and told her about their girls' abortions and their professors' fascist natures. But after the exams everyone scattered, off to man the current barricades or, like Ivory, to take up a three-year scholarship to South America to study folk art. Anna was alone when Theo was born, unvisited in the maternity hospital and uncherished when she came out of it. Theo suffered from a congenital disease, and she took him for repeated visits to the outpatients' clinic so that his tender skin could be pricked for samples, and prodded, and discussed over Anna's head.

The immigration authorities required to be assured quite often that the child was still in need of treatment. Anna had not, either by birth or marriage, a status or nationality which entitled her to stay in the United Kingdom. But the officials were not monsters; so long as the child was receiving medical care she could stay.

The man from the Department of Health and Social Security had also been trained in suspicion. Was Anna sure that she had no assets to realise? Nothing she could sell? This picture perhaps (one of Ivory's nudes)? Or Karl's radio? Or Anna's textbooks—they might have a secondhand value. Once the official came to call when Anna was unfolding the contents of the bag she had brought back from the launderette. Men's pyjamas? But had Anna not stated that she was living alone? Was she not aware that it would be an offence to claim benefits while she was cohabiting? Her lover would be deemed to be supporting her and the child. Frauds on the taxpayer, he must warn her, were taken very seriously. The man fingered the ragged pyjamas, and turned his gaze to the old slippers by the bed. "They are mine," Anna told him, and he replied, "They all say that."

Anna used to sit at her window staring at a stocking factory across the road where machinery thudded up and down all day and night, without stopping or varying its rhythm; there the noise was never less or more, and lights shone out through the tall windows for twenty-four hours a day. Slogans had been sprayed on the dark-red brick walls, between the windows: "BLACKS OUT," "COLOUREDS OUT," "NIGGERS GO HOME." Protesters marched down the street on Saturdays, on the way to the Town Hall. They demanded more welfare benefits, or fewer. One morning there was a new slogan on top of the others, in green paint: "SCROUNGERS, WE'LL GET YOU." It rained much of the time, rendering the dismal view even more so. Anna had constructed a detailed plan of where she would live one day, in a district of small hills and walled fields, with streams, thatched cottages and old grey churches. She thought it would resemble the map pictures of Tolkien's Hobbiton. Occasionally she dreamt of a less sober country, with heat, and monsoon rain, and drought; but for each sorrow, in that more violent land, a corresponding joy. From those dreams Anna always awoke to sorrow.

Anna was given money by clerks at the Social Security offices. Once a fortnight the ambulance called to take her and Theo to outpatients'. The little Indian boys in their spotless clothes would gather round to watch solemnly as she lifted the child in to join the other regulars—two old men, three older women, a youngish woman in a wheelchair. The street consisted of terraced houses on one side and the factory on the other. Nothing grew; the nearest blade of grass was the sparse vegetation on the banks of the canal which ran behind the stocking factory. The English boys were allowed to go fishing there, but the children of the immigrants were still homebound and obedient. Their parents told them, not to get out of the way, but to come indoors and be silent.

The rent was collected every week. Anna kept boxes on her mantelpiece into which she divided the money which she received. So much for rent, so much for putting into the gas meter. Theo's appetite was small, and Anna's vegetarian diet was not expensive. The meek women immured in the other rooms cooked spicy food, the smell of which made Anna's mouth water and reminded her of her childhood.

Theodore died at Christmas. Anna had pushed him to the market, so that she could see, through her invisible barrier of loneliness and disorientation, the ingredients of the jollity which other people were preparing. There had been office celebrations and lunchtime drinks. Clerks put up paper chains and stuck cotton wool and tinsel on the office windows. The man whose van mounted the pavement and knocked Theo's pushchair onto the road had no malice in him, unless drunkenness is a shout of defiance to the world.

Anna was given what the officials called a death grant to pay the expenses of his funeral. A few weeks afterwards, a bored, neutral, not unpleasant man saw her out of the country.

She arrived in Paris in midwinter; she had little luggage, for she had saved her money for the child. She was thin, with dull hair and a pale, chapped face, and she was mourning, inconsolably, the death of Theodore, her gift from God.

Karl's friends welcomed her without much interest. They were not sympathetic, for her experience was outside theirs; nor kind, for they did not believe in kindness; but they let her join their commune and wait for Karl to get out of prison. After so long a period of loneliness, that was a comfort in itself.

Karl behaved well in gaol, so as to get out of it quickly. He wanted to change the world while he was still young enough to enjoy inheriting the new one. He and his mates discussed numerous plans, grandiose and hopeless, or modest and hideously practical. Anna took them no more seriously than she had taken the gusts of invention he would puff out in the students' common room at Ferraby. At that time he was tipped as a future best-selling author.

Six years after that, in Paris, he had become a more earthbound man of action. He was crueller in intention, less ambitious in scope, more precise in his aims. Anna was at first dopey, during her second pregnancy; later, irrationally serene. She had closed her ears to discussions of death and, as she leant against Karl's warm strength, concentrated on the thought of a new life. She must have known that he was gathering money to buy their equipment. She must have heard the others discussing the relative merits of aiming at individual targets or inflicting random damage, planning the destruction of one society and their own parts in a new one.

It wasn't till after Billy was born that Anna had realised, or allowed herself to admit, that they truly hoped to spread terror from letters and parcels, and believed that bombs would create Utopia.

At one time the group had talked about coming to Britain. Most of them were prohibited immigrants, like Karl, and like Anna herself; but once they managed to get into the country they would be safe in the least regimented state in Europe, free to build their bombs without police searches, armed enemies, or identity cards.

Well, Anna thought, Karl had managed to get himself into the United Kingdom. She wondered whether the others were sticking it out in whatever squalid home they now shared, waiting to hear from him. They would have a long wait.

For the first time, as she thought back from her hard hospital bed to her old life, Anna wept for Karl's death, and not for her relief at it. She was crying not for the terrorist he had become, but for the enthusiast she had once loved.

The nurse came over and mopped her face with a tissue. "It's only weakness, dear," she told Anna. "I expect you're missing your little ones. Aren't they sweet?" She picked up the photographs, and gazed at Emmy and at Billy. He had wiry, copious curls, like Karl's, and dark, fierce eyes. He did not find life easy. Anna did not know whether she was crying for her dead husband or for her son.

CHAPTER 15

When James was still a woodwork teacher at a comprehensive school, living in an industrial town in Derbyshire
and spending his spare time at meetings of conservation
and preservation societies, he had been convinced that one
day Grebe would belong to him. Granny Wherry would
leave it to him because Simon did not want it, and Simon's
sister had opted for an urban life on the western coast of
America and did not want it either. James was so sure of
this that he had discussed his future plans for the estate
with many other people. It had been no secret that Grebe
was to become a reserve for natural life, free from develop-
ment, artificial methods of farming or chemical treatments
of the land and crops. He had given talks about his scheme
to enthusiasts, and written an article about it for one of the
best-intentioned, but perhaps on that account least efficient,
magazines about conservation. The delay in publication
was longer with each successive edition. On the day that
Anna was taken into Withiel Hospital, the article about
James's abortive plans was published, overdue by more
than two years. It made part of a longer piece about ecological salvation. Three places had been identified as sanc-
tuaries for the preservation of an uncorrupted environment.
In the intervening period, one of the sites had disappeared
under the tip of a newly opened colliery; the second was
the subject of a compulsory purchase order for an approach
road to a motorway extension; the third was Grebe.

Tamsin happened to be in River House, four days later,
when the postman arrived with a bagful of letters for
James. They were addressed to Grebe, near Withiel, but
the clerks at the sorting office had parcelled them together

and put a label under the string to tell the postman to deliver them to James at River House. James started to open them, and Tamsin picked up some of the letters.

"Those of us who foresee the impending ecocatastrophe would welcome the chance to join your scheme and live happily for the few remaining years of industrial so-called civilisation."

"We want to help you create a self-sufficient ecosystem," another enthusiast offered.

"Please send details of your planned return to historical methods of farming, with which humanity was happy until the disaster of the Industrial Revolution."

Tamsin read some of these effusions aloud. She exclaimed,

"Honestly, James, the dishonesty! Happy until the Industrial Revolution, indeed. The peasant labourer's life was worse than any farm animal nowadays. They were hungry, cold, ill, and died young. Do you believe all this? You couldn't if you've ever read anything about social history." She picked out some other letters, some written in beautiful italic script, others illiterate. Most were from people who thought they wanted to live primitive lives, but not without a bit of capital to help them along. "Listen to this one: 'Good luck to you in your one-man battle against this country's obsolete market mentality.'"

James leafed dejectedly through the letters and piled them into a shopping basket.

"I suppose they will have to be answered," he said. "Everyone means so well."

"Wait a bit, I should," Tamsin said, looking up from the article which had started it. "I expect there will be lots more tomorrow, and then for weeks while people get round to reading all this. Anyway, you may be able to start your commune after all now."

"Oh, that was a rather juvenile idea. I think Anna and I are too keen on our privacy now."

"Tell me, James," Tamsin asked, "were you going to reject penicillin for the children as well as weed killer for the fields? And immunisation from tetanus and polio? Or were you going to pick and choose the bits of modern civilisation you would let in?"

"Read more carefully. There never was any intention of resigning from the human race, only from the rat race."

"But then you would have lived the good life at the expense of the wage slaves who manufactured the parts you found acceptable. Technicians in drug laboratories, for instance. And who was going to do the hewing of wood and drawing of water in your Eden? Back to using women as beasts of burden while the men polish their souls?"

"We planned to have machinery which operates without wasting fossil fuels. It's called low-impact technology. Everything has been very carefully thought out."

"Including antidepressant drugs, like Anna's getting this very minute?" Tamsin jumped up, and flung the magazine onto the table. "Come on, James, I'll take the kids. I expect you've got heaps to do."

"It's very kind of you, Tamsin," he said, a little huffily. "As it happens, I've promised to take them out myself this morning. Another day it would be most kind."

Billy came in from the yard with a dried branch, and began to sweep the floor with it, scattering leaves among the crumbs and sticky stains. A column of ants was investing a slice of bread and honey on the floor under the sink. The cat was eating the baby's unfinished cereal. Tamsin opened her mouth to offer to clean up a bit, and closed it again.

"I am taking them over to Grebe, actually," James said. "I need to see what's going on there. Now, we know that Simon's dead . . . I hear the campers have all left since the body was identified."

"Did Simon make a will?"

"Granny said I was to have it if he died without making a will. I don't know whether he did. He wasn't very old."

"He has a sister, hasn't he?"

"Yes. She'd probably sell."

"Could you afford to buy it?"

"Oh, I don't know." James made a vague gesture, and

Tamsin said nastily, "There would be death duties." Being with James always made her feel like dressing in leopard skins or ostrich feathers, plastering her face with artificial substances, demonstrating into a real world which was cruel and money-loving, where people preferred adornment to the survival of a species. But she felt contented as she walked back to the cottage. Her feet flapped onto the rubber soles of her sandals, and the faint breeze caught under the skirt of her thin dress. She decided to get a floppy hat and a hammock.

James took the children across the river in his rowboat. Emmy was parcelled up in a sling which he carried on his back, and she gurgled as he swung himself backwards and forwards at the oars. Billy wore a life jacket and leant over to try to catch the ends of the oars. James had to shout at him before he would sit still.

Billy was a good walker when he was in a good mood, but Anna's absence had upset him and he trailed along scuffing his feet and whining. Eventually James picked him up, and walked along with one child on his back and the other against his chest. He put them both down when they reached the beach, and Billy ran down to the water at once.

It was Saturday, and the beach had few people on it. Saturday was the day for visitors to come and go, "changeover day." All the landladies and cleaning women in the county spent the day scurrying around to obliterate the traces of the previous week's visitors and prepare for the next. They laid in bread and milk, for self-catering tenants, and chops and Cornish cream for those who had booked evening meals as well as their bed and breakfast. Launderettes were crowded with those landladies who did not simply turn the sheets upside down and end to end.

James thought of the tanned families slogging through traffic jams back to the Midlands, and the pale, hopeful travellers on their way to crowd out his home. He detested them. He resented the litter and noise they scattered about them, hated the changes which were made in his county to accommodate them. He would have liked to pull up a drawbridge at the River Tamar.

James's eyes were darkened by an almost Pavlovian reflex when he observed that at the far end of his beach there was a large group of people with bedding rolls and other camping equipment. Simon had desecrated Grebe by turning it into a campsite. Now he was dead, it should be reconverted into a sanctuary.

Now he was dead. Dead, dead, Simon is dead. The words, spoken by the policeman, had come as a shock, brutal, loud, open. Simon, officially dead.

Dead; and yet James would miss him. An irritating, hostile, teasing, joking, offensive and overbearing relation called Simon Wherry had always been around, to be quarrelled with, to make up the quarrels with, to think of with shame, humiliation, hatred and, perversely, affection. To lose Simon was like losing a physical attribute—a wart or a mole. One was glad to be without it, but missed the identification it gave one's features.

Simon had been a part of James's life, a prop to his idea of himself. Simon learnt to ride a two-wheeler bike before James even dared to try one, but later it was Simon who skinned his knees and broke his collarbone falling off it, and James who went on camping holidays with his gear strapped onto the luggage-carrier. Simon told dirty stories and peered up girls' skirts while James was still hunting for birds' nests and building camps in the wood; but James had the first steady relationship with a girl. Simon was matey with the farmer and jocular with the farm labourers, but it was James they came to fetch when Granny slipped in the yard and sprained her ankle. One of Simon's girls had commented on the likeness between the two cousins. But Simon grew frown lines between his eyebrows and grooves beside his mouth, while James's face was still unmarked by experience or dissipation. When James was beginning to use a razor once a week, Simon had grown the masking facial hair which he cherished until he died. James grew a beard later, naturally. It would be a wicked waste of resources to shave every day, for even if the water was heated by the sun, and soap homemade, razor blades still consumed steel; but he kept his beard and moustache trimmed to a fringe around his mouth. Simon had got Grebe; but Simon brought Anna and James together. James realised that he was actually going to miss his cousin.

But as James walked along, automatically noticing the ravages of the drought, he was reminded that the long-term good of Grebe was assured by Simon's death. There would be no pop festivals, or campsites, or applications for planning permission. James knew, though he had not wished to admit it to Tamsin, that Simon never did make a will; at least, he had said, a few months before, that he had not done so—on one of the many occasions when he taunted James with his own possession of James's heart's desire. "Such a healthy life you lead," he'd said. "You ought to outlive me. Though whether you'll like the place you inherit will be another matter. It should be a good deal changed by then."

Well, Grebe had been preserved so far by luck; from now on, it would be judgement.

As James came nearer to the group of people whom he had intended to warn off the place, he saw that they were not the marauding tourists or careless campers he had so resented here before. These were his soulmates, his allies. Men whose hair was long on principle, not for defiance; girls who eschewed artifice because nature is beautiful. They wore the usual uniform, but it fitted badly, and on their canvas holdalls they had fixed their recognition signals—stickers about friendship to the earth, and making love not war, pleas to protect nature and destroy industry. Two of the girls had been swimming, and as they came out of the water they displayed their imperfect figures, being without pretence.

"Jimmy! It's us!" he heard a high voice call.

It was Maureen, the first woman who had ever made love to James, years ago, in the rooms of the Healthy Life Cooperative, when she was assistant editor and James brought in freelance contributions about lepidoptera. She had moved on to nuclear disarmament, after it had ceased to be a fashionable cause, and to political lobbying. Once her photograph, showing her bearing a banner and with a wide-open mouth, had been on the front page of the *Sunday Times*. She came forward and flung her arms around James. He felt her wet soft body against his without emotion.

"It's been so long, Jimmy. Years. We read your article and here we are. We have come to join you. Do you know Danny?" She dragged a small thickset man with pimples off the ground; he had been leaning against a backpack which had a long-handled shovel strapped to it.

"Peace to you," Danny said firmly. He shook James's hand vigorously. Several of the other people pressed forward, and another of the girls said, "We're the advance party. Larry's lot are hitching down after us. Marvellous news, that your work is starting; we were all so excited to read about it. I can feel the atmosphere here, the vibes, you know? Powerful emanations . . . earth influences . . . Atlantis . . ."

James interrupted her mystic burblings. "What do you mean about joining me, Maureen?"

"The commune, of course. Don't worry; we're all skilled. I pot, these days. There ought to be perfect clay in a place like this. Danny has a printing press, but he's willing to dig, as you see. Salome spins—lots of room for sheep, I see. We knew you would be pleased to have help."

"Who's Larry?"

"Oh, you remember Larry, Jimmy, don't you? Plays the guitar and the accordion. We need a few flowers of the field. But he can cook as well."

"Cook!"

"Aren't you pleased to see us? We're just what you need. It will be the best commune in Britain. We'll show them about self-sufficiency."

"But I don't . . ."

"We know all about it, you see; we've been living on a farm in the Welsh border country, but things have been getting a bit hairy recently with the landlord. He didn't understand our ideals. And then there was trouble with the local council—you know how it goes. That's why your news was so timely. Anyway, here we are. You tell us where to stake out and we'll set to work. I've walked over the place already, and I can tell you, Jimmy, it's just as well that we've turned up or you'll be stuck with those squatters."

"Squatters?"

"Didn't you know about them? There's about half a dozen guys and girls up by the house. They were all hunting for something when we went past. One was tapping on the cobblestones with a crowbar. Aren't they living there? I thought they were, didn't you, Danny? A girl with red hair and a chap with a beard and some others. They didn't look our sort, if you know what I mean. Actually, the girl was crying and saying that she wished they had never stayed here in the first place. Do you think they have been here since your Gran died? She said they should have moved on the moment they arrived. Not haunted or anything, is it?"

"I heard the tall chap telling her it was all her fault for letting Simon see the stuff in the first place," Danny said. "I don't know what stuff they were talking about. I suppose Simon is that cousin of yours, is he?"

"What else did they say?" James asked.

"Nothing much. We weren't really listening, just looking round. Something about Simon saying he'd give the stuff back when they left."

"I'm sorry for her," Danny said. "Poor kid, if she's desperate for a fix or something. Ought we to see if we can . . . ?"

"No, she's got her friends with her," Maureen said. "Anyway, they went off after they noticed us. They had a car; I thought it must be yours at first, Jimmy, it was so full of things like toys and sweetie papers and buckets and spades. Someone told me you had a couple of kids by now."

Billy had been playing by the water's edge, but he was getting hungry and came to stand beside James, pulling at his trousers and demanding something to eat. He looked unpleasantly at Maureen and then ran at her, butting his hard little head against her pubic bone. Maureen gave a forced laugh, and squatted down to look solemnly into the child's eyes.

"You'll want to do better things than hurt me there, one day," she said.

"You can't stay here," James said.

"But I thought . . ."

"My grandmother left the estate to my cousin. I don't live here."

"But the article we read . . ."

"That was written years ago. It's completely out-of-date."

"Oh, well." Danny shrugged his shoulders. "That's the way the cookie crumbles, as they say."

"Oh, Jimmy, how sickening." Maureen sounded like the girl she used to be for a moment, and James softened enough to explain.

"Simon's dead, as it happens. Recently. He was—"

"But that's marvellous. You'll be able to take over after all."

"I don't know about that. There are formalities . . . We weren't on the best possible terms."

"Oh." Maureen sat down on the sand, her knees splayed apart, her chin on her hands, and James felt a quick surge of gratitude for his graceful Anna. "I am not sorry we came, all the same. It's lovely here. You could have made it into a paradise."

"You will find somewhere else," James said, knowing that he never could himself.

"I guess we'll stick around. Okay if we camp up in that place by the house? It seems to be a good site."

James felt a violent revulsion against the thought of going up to the house, or seeing his former friends installed beside it. Had he really ever thought that his escape to Grebe would be in so much, and such, company? He fixed his mind on Anna and the children and his previous privacy. He said, "Oh, do as you like. It's nothing to do with me," and he and the children walked away across the beach.

CHAPTER 16

As Anna appeared to be getting better, people started to talk to her with more than the meaningless soothing she had received at first. She began to take in the sense of what they said. The doctor told her about hormonal imbalance and postnatal depression, and he discussed it, across the bed, with James. Lady Lurie came and said that it must be a relief for Anna to have handed over the struggle at home for a while.

"Just what you need," she said complacently. "Peace and quiet without the children, and meals on a tray put in front of you. You were worn out, my dear, by the struggle to feed the baby. I have always had my doubts about this modern emphasis on breast-feeding."

Tamsin came in, after several days, bringing peaches and plums to counteract the stodgy diet. She said, "They come from the health-food shop. They promised me everything is compost-grown, though I don't know how they can be sure." Tamsin chatted lightly about the weather—the third month of drought was now causing as much anxiety as pleasure, and those without piped water were beginning to be reduced to borrowing bucketfuls from their neighbours —the work she was doing, her own children, Anna's children. "Emmy's the sweetest baby, Anna. You are clever. I love little babies."

Anna was still under the influence of tranquillisers, though the dose was being gradually reduced. She listened to Tamsin and watched her animated face with a kind of abstract calm.

"You look like a madonna," Tamsin said suddenly. Tamsin herself looked the very opposite, with her untidy

clothes, wiry figure and hair, and busy gestures of hands
and face. The two women's reflections showed, side by
side, in the glass window of the ward, against the white
coat of a doctor who was chatting to someone on the other
side. Tamsin impatiently pushed her hair behind her ears
and pulled at her fringe. "I must get myself tidied up," she
said. "What Alex would think . . ."

They sat in silence for a while. Then Tamsin talked a little about her work. "I had to go and interview a farmer
about the dry weather. He had to plough a whole newly
sown field in, because nothing had germinated. And then
there was the music festival near Newquay . . . and the
sand-sculptures competition. Do you know anyone who
might unbutton about the row over the next mayor of
Withiel? Everyone seems scared to speak."

Anna sat placidly, smiling a little, like royalty at an
event of only minimal interest, formal, head a little on
one side.

"What else is there to tell you?" Tamsin went on, glanc-
ing surreptitiously at her watch. "I know. Did you hear
about that body Ben and I discovered in the river? I don't
know whether it's public knowledge yet, but it wasn't that
anarchist Karl Fischer after all."

Tamsin clapped her hand over her mouth. She had completely forgotten about Simon Wherry's relationship with
Anna.

"I don't know who it was," she said firmly. "I haven't
heard about that. Goodness, look at the time. I must go.
Lovely to see you so much better. You look better even
since I got here. See you."

After Tamsin had left, it was time for lunch. Later in the
afternoon, James would come with the children. Yesterday,
Billy had been noisy and wild, bumping into beds and
trolleys. He loved the way they moved smoothly on their
castors. When James had picked him up to prevent the
whole room turning into the sort of chaos usually created
by Laurel and Hardy, his screams had echoed through the
ward.

The lunch was some glutinous, adulterated substance,

chemically seasoned. Anna pushed it around on her plate and hid most of it under a slice of bread. After the trays had been taken away a nurse came round with a trolley of pills. Anna put the little blue bombs into her mouth, but held them against her cheek until she had locked herself into the lavatory cubicle, and then she spat them into the water.

This was supposed to be a time for resting. Some of the other patients were asleep, but most were in the day room watching a romantic film on television. Anna's jeans and shirt were folded on the lower shelf of the bedside locker. She emptied out the contents of her sponge bag and crammed the shirt into it. Her jeans she rolled inside her towel. She changed into her day clothes in the lavatory cubicle, and waited to unlock the door until it sounded as though there was nobody around. She had reached the swing door which opened onto the stairs when the staff nurse caught up with her.

"Now, Mrs. Buxton dear, what's this, then? Where do you think you are off to?"

"I have decided to go home."

"I know, my love, you're wanting to be with your family. The kiddies will be fine, I can tell you that much. You're ever so lucky; your husband is lovely with them. I don't know what would happen if I had to leave mine. But you haven't any call to worry. Why don't you come and watch the film with the other ladies?"

Imperceptibly, Anna was being drawn back into the main part of the ward, past the closed doors of the dressings cupboard, the sluice room, the open reception area, the glass doors into the day room. It was a place originally constructed for discipline, with high green walls striped with heating pipes, and bleak expanses of polished floor, but it had been cosied up with modern chairs and tables and a large television set, on which was an announcement that it had been donated by Friends of the Hospital Fund; on the tables lay tattered magazines, none less than three years old, and some small, unambitious pictures had been hung high up on the wall. Two women in dressing gowns were playing rummy at a coffee table. In the far corner of the day room, away from the noise of the movie, an elderly woman in tweeds and pearls sat weeping.

"I will not go in there," Anna said. "I have to leave; I must go."

"Let's have a word with Sister, shall we? I expect you could do with something to soothe you down."

"No, I won't take anything," Anna cried. The other patients were looking toward her, and a very small person whose mouth twitched all the time came and stood close to Anna, peering sideways up at her. "If I don't get away I really shall go mad. You can't make me stay here."

"Why don't we ring up your husband and see what he thinks? Maybe he'd like to come and have a word with Doctor."

"Look, you're trying to slow me down. I shan't wait until you get James here, and a doctor, and some more of your consciousness-lowering drugs. You have all been very kind to me." She detached her arms from the nurse's grasp, and pushed her hair back from her hot cheeks. "I haven't anything against you; I know you mean well and you have done your best for me. But you don't understand—nobody understands—I must go."

The ward sister came bustling up the corridor, and the nurse shrugged her shoulders and spread out her hands. There was more persuasion, identical argument, from the sister.

When Theodore was in hospital, as he frequently had been during his short life, Anna had grown to hate and fear the staff who looked after him. They had kept her out, in the dark, excluded from helping or knowing. She had felt all the time that it was love which would save the child. In the end, neither love nor skill had been enough.

Anna had never been near a hospital since that time, until being delivered to the psychiatric ward of Withiel Hospital. Billy had been born in the commune, with Karl kneeling beside her; Emmy was born at River House, in Anna's own bedroom, surrounded by the people and things she loved. Anna could not forgive nurses and doctors for keeping her away from Theo. She had read a novel in which a mother, similarly shut out, screamed until she was allowed to join her child. Anna had willed herself to do the same, and opened her mouth more than once, only to find that the long-nurtured inhibitions against sticking her foreign neck out, or raising her alien's voice, prevented any sound from emerging.

She opened her mouth now, for security had made her braver. But she closed it again just short of the satisfying shriek she would have liked to emit. One yell would be enough to justify them in forcing drugs down her throat or jabbing them into her veins.

Anna took a deep breath, and smiled at the two nurses.

"It's so kind of you to be concerned," she said. "I'm really grateful for the care you have taken of me. But I really have to be on my way."

"You'll have to sign a disclaimer if you discharge yourself," the senior nurse said bitterly. "We can't be held responsible. You'll have to sign a paper saying that we aren't obliged to admit you again, and that if anything happens to you it's your own fault."

"Wait for your husband to come, dear, do," the staff nurse pleaded. "He'll be home, I expect. I'll ring him right away." She marched quickly off toward the office, and Anna could hear the telephone being dialled.

"No, I shan't wait. I'm going now." Anna tore her arm from the grip of the ward sister. "You can't stop me." She escaped through the swing doors and down the stairs, three flights made of reconstituted marble, past the porter's lodge —a man's voice shouted something after her—and out into the street. The air fell heavily on her head and shoulders, and the light was dazzling. Her feet sank into the melting tar as she crossed the road, and loosened pebbles stuck to the soles of her sandals. She turned down an alley between two warehouses. She did not know this part of Withiel at all, but ahead of her was a glint of water and she supposed that if she followed the river she would reach the edge of the town, and then the road home. The alley came out at another warehouse, dating from the time when goods could be delivered to it by sea. It was an ancient and crumbling building, with wine crates and empty bottles stacked outside it. Ahead she saw a square opening in the rough wall, on to the river itself, presumably the unloading bay for freight. It was half tide. Two pairs of swans floated past, and in the hot silence she saw a water rat plopping onto the mud from a hole in the bank opposite.

Anna turned along the path which flanked the riverbank, if path it was. In many places it was barred by parts of other buildings, and she had to jump down onto the mud to get past. By the time she had reached the end of the row of warehouses her jeans and sandals were oozing unsavoury slime, but she was able to cross a parched, empty sports-ground and rejoin the road out of Withiel. An ambulance went by just when she was about to go through the gate onto the paved road, and she ducked behind the hedge which bounded the playing field in case its driver had been sent to look for her.

It was so hot, plodding along the road, that several times Anna wondered whether she would be able to make it. She walked on the grass verges or, rather, verges where there had been grass in other years. Now they were hard earth surfaces, patterned with litter and clumps of dry brown vegetation. Only thistles grew brilliantly green beside the dead flowers and dying turf. The leaves on the lime trees had kept their colour, but they were crinkled and curled at the edges. The atmosphere was heavy with dust.

Several cars overtook Anna; she forced herself along, sometimes stumbling into an uneven jog and then sinking back into the persistent placing of one foot in front of the other. Nobody stopped to offer her a lift, perhaps because of the caked mud on her trouser legs. It smelt of drains and graveyards.

At last Anna came to the entrance to her own drive. Since she and James had taken the property it had deteriorated. The wooden gate was propped permanently open against the hedge because its hinges had rusted off. Deep holes had developed in the tarmac. Sometimes James would fill them with spadefuls of pebbles and clinker, but they were quickly hollowed out again by car tyres. The drive was flanked by huge rhododendrons and hydrangeas. In the spring the grass at the edges was masked by crocuses and daffodils, but now it was shrivelled and straggling. It had survived in the shrubs' shade but, being uncut and unwatered, presented a degraded appearance to match that of its owner.

Anna walked softly past the cottage gate, for Tamsin could not be trusted not to whisk her straight back to hospital. She forced herself on with less effort now that she was so near the children and James. They would set off at once in the lorry. She would take any food she could find in the larder, and some fruit, and Emmy's bottles, which would be ready in the refrigerator. She wondered where the sleeping bags were, but remembered that the portable gas stove was in James's workshop, and reminded herself to take bottles of fresh water, and a saucepan to warm the baby's milk.

The front door was closed, but the children and James would be living in the kitchen and studio, and Anna went round to the yard. The lorry was not there, and Emmy's pram was not in its patch of shade by the garden wall, with a canopy over the sleeping baby. The only sign of children was Billy's tricycle on its side in the yard, and some nappies flapping, in the increasing breeze, on the line. Anna ran, stumbling over the uneven concrete, to open the back door. She almost fell into the kitchen. "James," she shouted. "James, Billy, where are you?"

She could hear nothing but the dripping of the tap. The feeling of an empty house was unmistakable, but Anna ran from room to room all the same. Everything was dreadfully messy—the beds not made, all Billy's toys lying on the floor where he had last flung them, Emmy's room stinking of ammonia and excrement because the lid was half off the bulging nappy bucket. The sitting room, too, was drearily squalid; dusty ashes from the wood fire had blown over the furniture, and the books and newspapers lay where Anna had last seen them days before. Used cereal bowls had been left on the floor among Billy's model cars, and Emmy had been sick, some time before, on the rug in the playpen. Anna picked it up and carried it out to the washing machine in the kitchen, but she found that it was still full of damp clothes which she had loaded into it in the previous week. When she opened the door, a smell of rubber and mould wafted out. Presumably, the nappies on the line had been rinsed out, inadequately, by hand.

Anna took some deep breaths and drank some water, appreciating its uncontaminated taste after the chlorinated liquid provided in the hospital.

James must have taken the two children for an outing in the lorry. Perhaps they had gone to the beach, or for a picnic up on the moor. When he returned, she would convince him that they should go away for a while. They could say they were having a holiday; perhaps go and stay at Penwith with Ivory Judd. Anna suddenly thought that Karl might be visiting Ivory Judd. They had all been friends, long ago. Could he have . . . ?

Anna went upstairs and fetched the sleeping bags and some blankets. She found a large cardboard crate in Billy's bedroom, and emptied the toys in it onto the floor. Down in the kitchen again, she loaded it with enough crockery and cutlery for a few days of camping. The cupboard was rather bare, but they could buy something on the way. She packed a jar of honey and took a couple of loaves and a dish of vegetable stew from the deep freeze. She wrapped the bottles of goats' milk which James had prepared for the day in damp paper, polythene and towels, and propped them upright in the box.

The camp stove had recently been on the workshop table, and she hoped to find matches there as well. She went out into the yard again. The wind had risen very quickly, and she had to screw her eyes up against eddies of dust. While she was standing with her hand on the handle of the workshop door, she heard the sound of a motor engine in the drive, and waited, much relieved, and unhysterically determined, for the lorry with her family in it to come round the corner into the yard.

CHAPTER 17

Mr. Quarles, the Home Office representative, was, as usual, finding it heavy going with the local police force. He ought to have been used to the suspicion and coldness he always encountered, but he still disliked it. He assumed it was because he had his powers without having had to put in years of pounding a beat. Inspector Gemmell thought the man was a supercilious bastard and had not given his training or qualification a thought. The Superintendent did not think it was a life for a white man, spending his days hunting down illegal immigrants.

The three men were sweating it out together in the conference room at the police station in Withiel. The curtains were drawn against the sun, but it was too windy to open the windows. Gemmell looked at the thermometer.

"Eighty degrees," he moaned. He twitched at the damp material of his shirt to peel it from his back. The Home Office man sipped tepid water from a paper cup.

"You're wasting your time, I can tell you that. Whatever was going on would have stopped the minute we got active about the Pakistani immigrants, and, as you know, there have been arrests in that case," the Superintendent said. "It's a chapter of errors, all on account of the mistaken identification. We can't be expected to make accurate identifications now that rich men like Simon Wherry go and buy their jewellery in junk shops. The sort of men who wear trinkets . . ."

"I beg your pardon, sir." Gemmell was embarrassed in front of the snooty bastard from London. If the Super would devote less of his time to having drinks with members of the Watch Committee, and making plans for his own retirement party, there would have been time to make a report on the information from Sir Arnold Lurie before this meeting.

"Wait a minute, Gemmell, let me finish. I want to explain to Mr. . . . er . . . I want to explain about the pathologist's report. You see, we needn't treat it as a case of murder after all. Once the body had been identified we could have a word with the man's general practitioner. It turns out that Wherry had a violent idiosyncrasy—what they call an allergy—against bee stings. He'd been in trouble from one before. Of course, once the pathologist knew what to look for, he could find what he needed at once. In effect, the man's throat swelled up and he died of suffocation. We shall be able to get the medic to tell the Coroner that the cause of death was almost certainly multiple bee stings, from which he died, and fell dead into the sea. As simple as that."

"Doesn't that leave a lot of loose ends?" Quarles said mildly.

Gemmell clenched his hands so tightly that if his nails had been longer his palms would be bleeding. Did the old fool take Quarles for an idiot?

"Sir, I haven't had a chance to tell you that the information from Councillor Mrs. Lumb, which you were inclined to discount, seems likely to be accurate after all. We have had a statement made by Sir Arnold Lurie—"

"What's that, Gemmell?"

"I am sorry, sir," Gemmell said stolidly. The Home Office man gave him the ghost of a wink, and Gemmell relaxed a little. If only it wasn't so damned hot. "Sir Arnold Lurie came with a recommendation from the Dep. Comm., sir. He's one of those old blokes who knows everyone. I told him a certain amount, that being so."

"I must have seen him," the Superintendent said. "When I was processing to the Civil Service with the councillors. He was coming out of here—an old image in bowler and brolly? In this weather! The holidaymakers gave way to him like royalty."

"That's the one, sir," Gemmell said, wondering how his

superior had ever been promoted. He ought to be bowler-hatted himself. He managed, in spite of the old man's self-glorifying interruptions, to relate what Arnold Lurie had told him about Anna Cohen, otherwise Fischer, otherwise Buxton. "So you see, sir, we must accept that Fischer had local connections. He may well have been here, staying at Grebe, as we were advised. Perhaps he was keeping an eye on his former wife across the water."

"Former wife, you think?"

"I can check on the place of divorce, I suppose, sir—whether it was here or in Europe. Certainly she and James Buxton got married here. I remember it. It was the day that Constable Grove—do you remember him, sir?—got hitched. I saw the Buxton pair at the registry office myself."

"If the ceremony of marriage was bigamous," Quarles remarked, "then Anna Cohen or Fischer is still a prohibited immigrant."

"That's as may be," Gemmell said. "But we have no evidence that she joined up with Fischer again after he left Britain. She may have been living anywhere—back home in Bangladesh even. Don't they let you get a divorce there by saying 'I divorce you' three times? Or even writing it on a scrap of paper and sending it through the post to your husband or wife? I suppose the English courts would recognise that kind of divorce."

"Get a copy of her marriage certificate and see how she described herself on it," the Superintendent said.

"I'll do that thing."

The men read through some of the papers stacked in front of them, piles of reports by constables on the beat, or records of telephone conversations, or irrelevant letters replying to irrelevant queries.

"If every piece of flimsy in this building exploded tomorrow I'd be a happier man," the Superintendent sighed, pushing his files away from him and running his hands through his hair. He had thick, bushy curls, only a little grey, and liked to draw attention to them.

Vain bastard, Gemmell thought. He said aloud, "I've been thinking something else, sir. The Buxton child, William, was about six months old when they moved into River House. We've had that from more than one witness— the estate agent, the removal men—it's one of those details that doesn't seem to matter when you're writing it down. Now, although James Buxton was well known in the neighbourhood, nobody has mentioned seeing the parents together before they moved in. I haven't heard anything about him having a girlfriend and a child before that . . ."

"That needn't mean anything. These young people nowadays, they don't bother anymore. Marriage and inviting the family friends, getting the toaster and the set of sheets—it's all gone. He was probably sharing some squalid pad with the girl."

"He taught at a comprehensive school in Derbyshire, sir, and the report doesn't mention any such setup."

"I don't know what things are coming to. We sent my own girl off properly, I'll say that. Lace dress, three-tiered cake, confetti. Set me back six months' salary. But there's no respect these days, no . . ."

"No sir. I mean, yes, sir," Gemmell said doggedly. "But the point is—"

"Get on with it, man."

"If the child is not actually James Buxton's . . ."

"He should worry. They don't care for marriage or the blessing of the Church or how many men have been through their girlfriends before they settle down; long-haired layabouts, they just live for—"

"Look, sir. The child is described as dark, with black eyes and curly hair. Now, James Buxton has straight red hair, a pale complexion and light eyes. Mrs. Buxton is very blonde, described as having remarkable blue eyes."

"Didn't you tell me she came from India?"

"Bangladesh. But her father's family were from Eastern Europe—Germany I think, or Poland—and the mother's family was all British by descent."

"So?"

"I think it's possible that Karl Fischer is the father of the child known as William Buxton. He's a dark man."

"What does she say?"

"I told you, sir, I haven't been able to speak to her yet. She's been under sedation in Withiel Hospital for the last four days."

"That's another thing," grumbled the Superintendent. "All this psychological mumbo-jumbo. In my day it would have been called an attack of hysterics and she'd have been shaken out of it good and proper. We didn't have time for anxiety states and postnatal depression. I'd give her anxiety states."

Inspector Gemmell had a calendar at home on which he was ticking off the days until the Superintendent's retirement. There were precisely one hundred and nineteen to go. He reminded himself of how the red marks were gradually covering the page. "I'll try whether they will let me in today, sir. But the point I'm trying to make is that, if the child is Fischer's, that might explain why he was here. Perhaps he wanted to get his hands on the infant. So what I thought was—" He spoke rapidly, before the old deadbeat could interrupt again, "If we were to keep observation on the little boy we might find Fischer coming back to get him."

The Home Office man made a "thumbs-up" gesture at Gemmell. "That's the stuff." He turned his mild gaze back to the Superintendent. Gemmell decided that he wasn't as bad as he'd thought at first sight.

"Would you like to come with me?" he said. "I'll show you round a bit, let you have a gander at the territory."

Quarles spoke for the third time that afternoon. "Lead me to the cold beer," he said.

CHAPTER 18

Pippa and Ben had set off on their much-discussed, long-planned school outing. Carrying their picnic teas, they had joined the crocodile of children from the top two forms of Withiel Primary School. They were to celebrate the end of the school year with a picnic at Grebe. Mrs. Potter, who was Ben's form teacher, had got the idea for the expedition from hearing Tamsin's mention of the Large Blue Butterfly on the radio.

"But I never said where," Tamsin protested, her voice rising above the buzz of the parents and teachers at an association meeting. She felt guilty on account of James.

"No, but knowing you, and knowing the district so well, I could easily work it out. The children are very excited. We have fostered a real enthusiasm for natural history at this school."

The school hall was decorated with posters showing slowworms and adders, toads and bullfrogs. "Of course, I didn't tell the children where we would be going. Though I daresay I could have trusted them. We have our less cooperative elements. No, it's to be a surprise outing for the end-of-term treat. Such fun we'll have, a real treasure hunt —with notebooks and cameras, naturally, no butterfly nets. We'll take our snacks—crowst, as we say here—and see whether we can get the name of Withiel Primary into the natural-history books. Isn't that a lovely idea?"

Tamsin watched the children as they went along the river footpath. Across the mud and water came the slightly dispiriting sound of their voices singing, to the tune of "The Wizard of Oz," that they were off to find the butterfly, the wonderful insect of Grebe. They would not be back until early evening, when the children who lived on the south side of Withiel would be allowed to peel off from the school party and make their own way home. Tamsin was relieved that the children would be out late. Pippa, especially, had displayed an irritating and ingenious form of hatefulness since Alex came. He had told her that the divorce judge would ask which parent she wished to live with, and, although Alex must have made it clear that he and Clarissa did not want to take her to America, she had got into the habit of, as she thought, threatening Tamsin with an adverse decision.

Since the term was nearly over, Tamsin wanted to clear up quite a lot of work this afternoon. She gave her father coffee when he dropped in on his way home after the London trip, and had only just settled down at her typewriter when James appeared on the doorstep, looking haggard and harassed, and begged to be allowed to dump the children on her for a little while.

Tamsin tore her mind away from the search for a precise word, the one which would describe the smell, or feel or emanation, of the book she hoped to start after the holidays. She had woken one morning with a set of characters formed in her brain. She was going to write a novel about a woman who knew what she wanted and got it; it would be concrete and precise, not, like the three earlier books, impressionistic and tentative. She tried to fix the half-formed thoughts onto her memory, and James dumped the carrycot on the floor, pushed Billy into the room, and backed quickly out, before Billy could set up his usual protest at being left.

Billy made for the typewriter and started to press the keys and rub his fingers over the inky letters. Emmy was making fractious noises. Her skin felt clammy when Tamsin picked her up, and Tamsin hoped that she was suffering from nothing worse than the heat. The shapes of teeth bulged through her gums, and Tamsin said, "There, there, poor teething baby." Alex used to hate it when she spoke a special language to their babies. Clarissa would probably call them "diddums."

Tamsin carried the cot out to put it onto the wheeled base, and told Billy they would go for a walk. He began to cry, but they walked out of the drive onto the road, and over to look at the water and the boats bouncing up and down in the increasing breeze. The *Cock's Comb* was neatly battened down. The sails were furled round the boom and encased in a canvas tube, and a green tarpaulin cover was stretched over the cabin roof. She wondered who had tidied the boat up, and to whom it now belonged.

"Hullo."

Tamsin turned round to see a man kneeling beside Billy in the dust. Beside him stood the red-haired girl whom Tamsin had once seen with Simon Wherry. The little boy was usually shy, but he stared solemnly into the man's face without flinching.

"Hullo," the man said again. "You must be Billy."

CHAPTER 19

Anna saw that it was not James driving in the yard in his lorry, but Karl Fischer, dressed like a paterfamilias on holiday and driving a car either stolen or copied from one, festooned with toys and dangling monkeys and packets of sweets. No policeman would have given him a second glance.

He was alone. He stopped the car inside the arched gateway and got out to stand beside her.

Anna knew she would have to see him in the end; it was almost a relief that the moment had come. She was still clutching the handle of the workshop door, and for a second she felt the impulse to embrace him and let his strength take her weight. Once upon a time she had married him for love. She was glad, after all, that he was not dead.

He watched her warily at first, but quickly saw that she was not going to run for it, and said, "Isn't he here? I came to see him."

"James? No. He's out, with the children."

"Ah, yes. The children." He took her hand, unfolding it from the doorknob and looking at its cracked, chapped fingers, and then he put his hand into his pocket, still holding hers, so that she felt the rough texture of the fabric at the back of her hand, and the strong, hard warmth of his palm against hers. Against her knuckles was another bulge, and she was reminded of happy nights, and how in Ferraby, she had pined for them.

Karl steered Anna towards her own garden, and sat down close to her on a wooden bench which James had made from a fallen chestnut tree. Anna stared at the ground, at the wood lice running from under the flowerpots and at the ladybirds, present in multitudes that year, and at the yellow lichen on the stone urns in which she was growing scented geraniums. Their leaves would be used in September to flavour the blackberry jelly, and she would take cuttings of them to have in the house in the winter. She tried to steady her mind with thoughts of the good life she had created.

"Well?" Karl said.

"What?" she answered, not lifting her eyes, and he grasped her chin in his thin, strong fingers to turn her face towards his. There were new lines etched horizontally across his forehead, and in his newly trimmed beard white streaks stood out against the dark brown. His eyes were as black as olives.

"You have done very nicely for yourself with my money," he said meditatively. "Very bourgeois. Do you know how I've been living since you took it that day?"

She shook her head.

"It was stupid of me," he went on. "I thought you had just gone down to the town to buy something for Bilbo. It was Myra who kept saying that you must have run out on us. And then we saw that there weren't any tyre marks, and we realised you had left in the evening, before it had started to snow. So there we were."

"I was sure you would manage to get a lift," Anna muttered. She twisted her lips at the memory of her flight through France, when every car on the road behind her seemed full of revengeful followers.

"So we might have got a lift, if the police hadn't got us first."

"Oh no, Karl."

"Oh yes, Anna. The police and Customs people are very suspicious so near to the Andorran border. All those tourists buying cheap alcohol. So they came in, smelt the smoke, had a search, and there we were on our way back to prison. Another eighteen months all round."

"I don't know what to say."

"Try apologising, why don't you? Anyway, we're back in

business now—more than ever, actually. The equipment has been sophisticated in the last two years. We've got a marvellous new timing device. Myra heard about it when she was in the nick. Or rather—we had one."

"Are you really still set on revolution? Yes, I can see that you are. You'll do anything, no matter how dreadful, to change the world, won't you, Karl, even though nobody wants you to? James can't bear things the way they are any more than you can, but he doesn't want to bully other people. All he wants is a decent corner for his family."

"Yeah, I know. You should have heard what his cousin thought of him."

"Thought?"

"Well, he's dead, isn't he?"

"Dead? Simon. D'you mean—?"

"Well, whose did you think that corpse in the river was?"

"We were told it was yours."

"That's what we hoped people would think. But it was Wherry. Tell the truth, I wondered whether it was you that killed him, you or your precious James. But he wouldn't have had the nerve. Now, in your case, Annie, it's quite different. Isn't it?"

"What are you talking about?"

Karl gave Anna an edited version of events. He did not tell her that he could easily have killed Simon Wherry himself. He had been an unbearably annoying man.

When Wherry first discovered what his guests were up to, Karl had been amused by the sophistry which enabled him to justify his own profitable but illegal trade in prohibited immigrants, while becoming moralistic and self-righteous about the unlawful actions of Karl and the others. He had lectured them about the differences between moral and administrative law, acts which were wrong in themselves and those which only transgressed regulations. He told them that it was no crime to ignore artificial national boundaries.

The poor guy didn't know what he had got himself into. He had taken a tiger by the tail, thinking it was a domestic cat. So blind was he to the realities of other people that he had accepted the whole gang at face value. He believed what they told him: that they were Commonwealth citizens who just wanted to have some fun in the old country and were excluded by idiotic legislation. Simon was still angry when he remembered an episode at London airport years before when he had been grilled by a passport official whose accent and skin betrayed him as a first-generation immigrant, and felt no guilt about his profitable, illegal ferry service.

He had pressed them all to stay on at Grebe and fed them on gin and whisky. They had all enjoyed living his idle life in the sun, but they should have known better than to stay. Simon only realised that he had misinterpreted his visitors' intentions when he came across Myra using his kitchen table to pack one of her letter bombs. And Myra should have known better than to take his silence for interest or approval. The silly girl happily showed him everything.

Simon had tried to get rid of the whole gang. He'd whined that they had no right to use his place as a bomb factory, and said they had cheated him. He even tried a few threats, but he laid off that quickly enough when it was pointed out that he was hardly in a position to hand his own illicit passengers over to the authorities. Then he tried appealing to their better natures; that was the occasion when James Buxton had interrupted them. He had reminded Karl of a crooked businessman caught at the wrong end of a deal.

In retrospect, Karl was still staggered, still almost incredulous, that Simon Wherry had so much as dared to touch, let alone hide, the vital equipment. He had apparently watched Myra go off in the car with Karl to post a lethal envelope. They were going to drive as far as Plymouth, so that they would seem to have come on a day trip from France.

It was Ernst who met Simon, on the path down to the *Cock's Comb*. Karl tended not to take much notice of Ernst. He resented the way that Ernst, von und zu-something-or-other, would wince at the long vowels and aspirated sibilants of the orphan from Bavaria, when in heated moments they spoke their native language. So Karl didn't think it mattered when Ernst told him about meeting Simon. Simon had said, "You'll be leaving soon, I expect. When you do, I'll return your stuff."

Ernst had watched him row across, seen the door slam on a fragment of his blue shirttail. And they had not given him another thought until two days later when Myra noticed that her things were missing.

Karl had gone over to the boat, never dreaming that Simon was still there. He merely hoped to find the stolen goods.

The smell was unpleasant as he approached the boat, and the cabin door hard to open, for it had an automatic closing mechanism inside it. The blue shirt fabric was still protruding through the crack.

Simon's body had decomposed rapidly in the heat. It lay sprawled half on the bunk, half on the floor, covered with a layer of alive and dead insects. The surfaces in the cabin were sticky to touch, and there was a persistent buzzing and humming from the flies and bees. Karl's mind had dwelt on multiple murders for years, but he had never seen a corpse. Still, after the first nausea, he had planned his actions with the requisite coolness.

Identifying features were obliterated as far as possible—fingerprints, a mole on the neck, a scar on the wrist. An identity bracelet which would eventually be traced to Karl himself was fastened round the ankle. The *Cock's Comb* was sailed out of the Brann in the dark at high tide, and the body dropped into the ocean when they were miles away from land. A cleaned and disinfected yacht was returned to her moorings, and plans made for an indefinite stay, unchallenged, at the convenient headquarters of Grebe, with the use of the house, the car and the boat.

It was pure bad luck that the body came straight back. None of them could have known that it would do so, though Simon Wherry himself could have warned them of that unfortunate habit of the currents and prevailing wind. The whole affair had been dogged by too much bad luck.

Karl was surprised to find himself prepared to forgive Anna her share in it.

He told Anna what he had done with the body and, though her face grew even paler than it had been, she sat still and listened to him. He explained that he wanted James to do something for him.

"He never would!" she said.

"I expect we'll be able to persuade him. No offence, Annie, but he's a bit wet, isn't he?"

"No! He's good—a good man and a good father."

"You haven't given me a chance to be a father at all."

"Oh God," she said. "How did you ever find us here?"

"You shouldn't have given Simon the idea of ferrying passengers. That's how I came to be right here—so it's your fault. He's been making his living ever since he brought you over, by ferrying New Zealanders and South Africans— guys who don't have work permits. I was told about Simon by about five sources. He'd built up a steady trade. He was only boarded once that I know of, which was the time he had Myra on board, and of course he just said she'd sailed out of Grebe with him and they were on the way home again."

"He's been doing this for two years?"

"That's right. But he had to pack it in after those Pakis-tanis—"

"You didn't—oh, Karl—?"

"No, nothing to do with Simon. Pure coincidence, but it made it dangerous to carry on. We had to turn back one day when the patrols were out. That's why I'm dependent on the supplies we already had in the country."

"You aren't still living at Grebe?"

"We had to move out. Can you imagine, a revolution foiled by a sanitary inspector! Luckily, the day the police first came only Myra was around and she managed to fool them."

"Why are you here, then?" Anna said, terrified to hear his answer.

"I want something of you and James. Why do you think?"

"No," she cried. "Not Billy. You can't." She stared at his

inscrutable face and wondered how it could ever have represented happiness. He didn't care about people; he didn't care about world revolutions. He just cared about his own revolution. And Anna knew that he would never succeed in anything he planned. The worst he would do was cause random misery and, in her case, cause particular, directed doom to her peaceful world.

If only he had not gone to Paris, all those years ago, she thought. If he had stayed with her, Theodore would have turned him into a feeling, compassionate man. Theodore might even still be alive.

"How's my son?" Karl said suddenly. She made a sharp gesture, shrinking herself into the protection of her folded arms.

"I knew it," she murmured. "I knew it."

"Good-looking little chap," he said.

"You've seen him?"

"What are your plans for him?" he asked, with no aggression in his voice. "I really want to know."

"He is to grow up in a stable world," she said, emboldened by despair. "I want him to know that life will be the same tomorrow as yesterday. I don't want him to know about fighting and hatred. I want him to live as part of nature's cycle, see living creatures grow from youth to age, from birth to a natural death. He's not going to live in a garret while his father plans murders. He's not going to live with insecurity."

"The revolutionary's child!"

"He's going to have a better life than the revolutionary's first child ever did," she shouted. She added, more gently, "I learnt a lesson. Billy and Emmy are going to grow up safe. James and I will protect them."

"And happy?"

"And happy. We shall lead the life we have chosen because it is good. Nobody will interfere; nobody will stop it. I shall ensure that, no matter what I have to do."

"You'd commit murder for it?"

She looked at him thoughtfully. "I would commit murder for it, yes. And I would certainly condone it."

CHAPTER 20

As the tall man followed Tamsin into the cabin, his stooped head rested cheek to cheek with the little boy in his arms. The likeness between them was very marked. She looked from one black curly head to the other, and compared their smoothly down-curved noses. The man grinned, with Billy's grin.

"You see why I said that I won't do you any harm," he said.

The little room smelt of chlorinated scouring powder and engine oil. Karl Fischer put Billy gently on the floor. Although it was still brilliantly sunny, the wind was rising and the water under the boat was choppy, so that Billy stumbled and bumped onto the floor. "You okay, mate?" Karl Fischer said. Billy stared at him without making a sound, but he did not seem frightened by the unknown man who had forced him and the baby and Tamsin to accompany him to the *Cock's Comb*. "Your mum will be here soon," the man said. "And you, Tamsin? Yes, Tamsin, don't try to make a noise or anything, will you? My friend will be sunbathing on the roof." He knocked with his knuckles against the ceiling and was answered with a triple knock from above. "She doesn't have any special reason to be nice to these kids, unlike me. The reverse, in a way. So I wouldn't annoy her, if I were you." He backed out of the cabin door, which fell heavily closed behind him. Tamsin heard a bolt slide across, and a key turn in the padlock.

The heat in the cabin became almost unbearable very quickly. Tamsin took off all Emmy's clothes except her nappy. Billy would not let her remove his cotton shorts or shirt. He rushed around opening all the cupboards and jumping on the bunks for some time, but then he curled up on the floor and sucked his thumb. His face was pale, and Tamsin wondered whether he would be sick. She ran some brackish water from the tap and wrung her handkerchief out in it to wipe his face, but he pushed her away and curled up more tightly in his foetal position. Tamsin tried to run some more water, but the tank must have been empty; a few drips fell from the tap, and then came nothing except some gulping sounds of air in the pipes.

She tried to see the land from the porthole, but a tarpaulin was hanging down over it; below the green canvas she could just see a section of the busy, dazzling water.

There were two tins of Coca-Cola in one of the overhead lockers, which otherwise contained only blankets and pillows. Tamsin drank some of the fizzy liquid. Billy spat out his first mouthful, saying it was sharp. He had never tasted it before.

After they had been in the cabin for about an hour, Emmy woke up and began to wail. Tamsin rocked her in her arms and the baby turned her lips to Tamsin's breast in reflex action.

Emmy's frantic crying had been joined by an awakened, miserable Billy's, when the cabin door opened again and Anna edged in through the gap. Billy rushed to her and flung himself violently against her. Karl Fischer's arms appeared through the half-open door, and put a large cardboard crate on the floor. It said "BRITISH FARM EGGS" but seemed to be packed with camping equipment. Anna soothed Billy, and sat down with one arm around him, while she cradled Emmy in the other.

"There is a bottle in the box," she said. "Can you get it?" Tamsin unwound the wet newspaper and handed the bottle to Anna. Although it was unheated, Emmy drank the milk eagerly. Billy sobbed for a longer time, but at last he too was quiet, and lay against his mother with his damp cheek resting against her arm.

Anna's face was as white as the milk in the bottle, and her hair stuck in sweaty strands to her forehead. Her eyebrows were raised, as though by stretching her eyes she would prevent tears from forming in them. Tamsin did not know how to speak, but the expression on her face was question enough.

"He wants to make James do something for him," Anna said. "He's telling him that we . . . James must do it or . . ."

"He would not hurt you," Tamsin said, with her eyes on the little boy.

Anna did not answer, but her arms tightened round the children.

"What does he want James to do?"

"Show him Simon's hiding place. Find something Simon stole from him."

"But what if James doesn't know?" Tamsin cried. "What if he can't find it? What is it, anyway?"

Anna bent her head so that her face was hidden. Tamsin walked, her head bent to clear the low ceiling, the two paces up and down the little cabin, backwards and forwards. It was becoming difficult to keep her balance as the water under the keel grew deeper. The waves slapped against the hull and the wind in the rigging howled noisily. After a while Tamsin sat down again and said, "You know I liked this boat when Simon took me for a sail in her. Funny . . . he said that 'Cock's Comb' means 'Grebe.' It's like the Black Hole now."

"Simon died in here," Anna said.

The two women looked around their cell. The *Cock's Comb* was an old boat which Simon had bought second-hand and refitted. The cabin was furnished with mahogany edged with narrow brass strips, with recessed brass handles, badly tarnished, on the locker doors. The floor was made of strips of some paler wood. Every corner was equipped, so that there was no wasted space. Somebody had been cleaning with scouring powder and wire wool. There were light-coloured scars and fine scratches on the surfaces, which Simon had always kept shining and polished. Tamsin restlessly opened and closed the cupboards, into which she had already looked before Anna arrived. "It looks as though bees have been nesting in here," she said. "Dead bees all over the place—look, in these blankets, and under the bunks. It's sticky there too."

Water from the waves splashed up against the deck. The tarpaulin over the cabin roof was wet, and under it drips of water ran down the glass of the porthole.

"Simon was allergic to bees," Tamsin said slowly. "If he had come into the cabin, smelling of whisky as he usually did, and found that a swarm of bees had somehow got in here . . . They get angry when they are disturbed anyway, and they can't bear the smell of alcohol. I wonder . . ."

Billy began to wail again, and Anna rocked the children backwards and forwards. Her wide lips were sucked in together, and her eyes stared blankly at the segment of water visible under the covering of the window. She still did not answer.

CHAPTER 21

Quarles of the Home Office had looked around the area with Inspector Gemmell and then gone on to pay a call on Sir Arnold Lurie. Lady Lurie brought them iced tea in the garden, and they sat in the shelter of a windbreaking trellis, and squinted at the dancing boats and the water scintillating in the late afternoon sun.

"You must be glad to have left London for this, sir," Quarles said.

They exchanged the requisite civilities for a short while, and then Sir Arnold said, "I suppose you're here about the Fischer business?"

"That's it, yes. The local police passed on to me what you were able to tell them. Things have been very slack down here. This illicit immigration may have been going on for months, if not years. There is a good deal of tidying up to do."

"Difficult, of course. Look at those craft down there. Half of them could cross to France and bring a passenger back without anyone being the wiser. What makes us so sure that Simon Wherry was the only one to think of it? The same thing could be going on at half the marinas and harbours along the south coast."

"I am afraid you may be right. But wouldn't you have thought someone would notice?"

"They might notice coloured people. But the 1971 Immigration Act excludes so many nonpatrials from the Old Commonwealth whose motives for illegal immigration are quite different. They don't feel they are doing anything wrong; they think they have a right to come in. Well, Quarles, you know the position as well as I do."

"At least things have been a bit better policed since that last lot of Pakistanis was washed up, poor chaps. It's made them more alert."

"I heard there have been arrests?" Sir Arnold said.

"Yes, the chaps who set them adrift were picked up in Belgium—some Dutch, Flemish and British, with a couple of fishing boats and a whole network of contacts in Brussels and Antwerp. If the survivors will give evidence, we may be able to get a murder charge to stick."

"Well, that's something sorted out. But I am afraid, Quarles, that illegal immigration may be the least of our worries in this case. I suppose you know the position about Karl Fischer?"

"Yes, I have been with the police in Withiel, sir, as I mentioned. They hope to be able to pick him up if he gets into contact with his former wife."

"They are so slow. To think of him wandering around the country all this time. He should have been recognised. I'm sure he will have gone to ground in a big city by now. He'll be able to hide indefinitely."

Quarles hesitated, and then said, "Why are you so worried about him? Is it because of Anna Buxton? Because, after all, Fischer is only an agitator, isn't he? As far as I know, he hasn't done any practical damage? Except, perhaps, to Wherry."

"I am not really sure myself why I am worried," Sir Arnold admitted. He stared frowning at the younger man. "I feel uneasy about it. I'd like to be sure what their purpose was in entering the United Kingdom. Incompetent as they undoubtedly are, they must have something in mind."

"You don't have any idea . . . ?"

"I imagine that Fischer has told himself that he has been holding his fire for a great day. *Der Tag.*"

"I wouldn't have thought that you need worry, sir. We see so many of these self-appointed saviours. If we worried about every one of them . . . You said yourself that they were incompetent."

"Yes. But, you know, if they have a target and a weapon, I agree with you that they are likely to miss. What worries me is whom they will hit by mistake, the harm they may do to some innocent bystander. They must have something in mind. I wish I could be sure what it was."

Inspector Gemmell shared Sir Arnold Lurie's anxiety, though for a more personal reason. He did not want the police forces of Europe laughing at him for letting Fischer slip through his fingers. He was convinced, whatever the pathologist had said to the Superintendent, that Fischer had something to do with Simon Wherry's death. He was bitterly humiliated at the thought of the traffic in illicit immigrants which had been going on literally under his eyes; he had himself seen what he had supposed to be the rich young bachelor's water parties on the yacht as it sailed in and out of the Brann.

Gemmell had stationed a constable at the entrance to River House's drive. He reported that the house and the cottage were deserted, although Tamsin Oriel's car was parked in the lane, and she had presumably only gone out for a walk. James Buxton and his children were out, but the hospital porter had said that Buxton had arrived there and been too late to catch his wife. The lorry was in the hospital car-park, and it was assumed that James Buxton had set off on foot to follow Anna and try to catch her on the way home.

Gemmell knew that if Fischer had had the luck of the devil he might have got at the woman, or the child, before the police watchers were in position. On the other hand, there was no reason to suppose he knew that he was suspected. Gemmell told himself that the Buxton children were almost certainly out with Tamsin Oriel. Soon they would come back for tea, James and Anna Buxton would arrive back together, and all would be sorted out. Only his instinct, not his reason, told him that he should be keeping a lookout. The Superintendent, who did not accept Gemmell's deductions, had not been told his fears, and was operating under a staff shortage, was being uncooperative about the whole thing.

It should have been Gemmell's afternoon for getting

home early. He had promised to take his wife over to see the sand yachting championships. Instead, he was waiting in the woods which separated Grebe from the outskirts of Withiel, above the bridge at the head of the river. He was sitting on soft moss, and cool now in the sharp breeze. He had kept observation in much worse places than this. He shifted his position and sighed, and fixed his attention firmly on the road to River House.

Karl Fischer had seen James Buxton as he came out of the sports-ground which Anna had crossed earlier in the afternoon. James had not followed the route she had taken along the river, but had walked the direct way, through the industrial part of Withiel and then across the large council estate. He had made several detours to look along the roads which ran parallel to his, because he was anxious to catch Anna, who, he had been told, was in a bad state. He had looked into the sports-ground, in case Anna had gone in to sit on the grass; he did not think she was strong enough to walk all the way home. As he came out of the gate, he was accosted by Karl Fischer. James did not know him, though his face seemed oddly familiar. Karl did not explain his relationship with Anna, but he went with him when Karl explained what he was to do, and what would happen to his family if he refused.

James said that he did not know where Simon would have hidden anything. But Karl Fischer drove him to Grebe in the stolen car, and had it parked behind the closed doors of the tractor shed before Inspector Gemmell's watchers were in position.

There were noises coming from the field beyond the orchard, where Karl's camp had been.

"You've got squatters," Karl said.

"How do you know that Simon hid whatever it is you have lost?"

"I know," Karl said. "And you had better find it, for your own sake."

"Have you looked in the house?"

"All over, unless you have a priest's hole or secret passage."

"None that I ever heard of. How big is the thing, anyway?"

"About so big, I guess," Karl said, spreading his arms.

"It could be anywhere, then. How should I know what he did with it? In an old haystack, or a shed . . . I don't know . . . What is it, anyway?"

"Mind your own business."

"That is all I have ever wanted to do. But how can I even think, when you have Anna and my children—what have you done with them?"

"They will be quite all right. Just you do what I want."

"If you had left them alone I might have helped you willingly. How do you expect me to think straight when I don't know they are safe?"

"You never will know that until you find Simon's hideout. You know this place better than anyone. Anna's got enough food for a while, for Bilbo and your baby, but I wouldn't dawdle too much in your position."

"Have you looked in the boat?"

"It isn't there. It has to be somewhere here."

Karl Fischer stood idly, with his hands in his pockets and his feet scuffing the ground. In the days since James had last been at Grebe the weeds had grown and brownish fronds of vegetation almost covered the cobblestones in the yard. In the garden the ground was cracked and dusty, and the house, too, looked degraded. James wondered whether it could ever recover from the summer's neglect. He said, "What did Simon hide your stuff for, anyway?"

"To get a hold over us," Karl answered. "He was that sort of a twister."

"I thought you were his friends."

"You thought wrong, then." The men stared at one another with mutual dislike. Karl thought that James was even more pathetic than his cousin Simon. He decided that it was out of the question to leave Bilbo to be brought up by him. James had not made the connection between Billy's beloved features and this man's. James said suddenly, "How do I know you've got Anna and the babies somewhere? For all I know, they are safely at home."

"Are you going to gamble on that?" Karl asked.

"No. No. I'll have to try to do what you want."

CHAPTER 22

After the point of high water, when the tide had turned, the boat rocked a little less, although it was still very windy. One of the lashings which held the tarpaulin over the cabin roof had worked loose, and the metal eyelet on the corner rapped irritatingly against the glass of the porthole.

"I suppose there really is someone on the roof," Tamsin said. She pressed her nose against the glass. "What if I tried to break it?"

Anna pulled her back. "Don't, don't. You don't know what kind of people . . ."

"No, well, of course you know about that better than I do," Tamsin agreed. "Why don't you tell me about them?" she went on, after a long pause. "Of course, I know that your—that Billy's father is what they call an international anarchist, whatever that may be."

"Don't call him that!"

"What? Billy's— All right. Does James know about him? No? Oh, Anna! Okay, tell me about Karl Fischer. What does he do? Chuck bombs around?"

Anna gave a stifled cry and clapped her hands over her mouth.

"What, really?" Tamsin said. "Come off it, Anna. I don't believe it. He isn't dynamic enough. I suppose he might post off letter bombs, which is bad enough, goodness knows, but by modern standards that is almost kids' stuff."

Tamsin was chattering to stoke up her own courage. The long confinement was getting her down; at first she had been inclined to treat it as some sort of practical joke, for the only inducement to make her go to the boat with

Fischer and Myra had been, quite simply, that Myra was holding Emmy, and Karl had said, in a mild voice, "Babies are so vulnerable, aren't they?" Now Anna's terror was infectious.

"At least Fischer didn't murder Simon," Tamsin said. "My father called in earlier and told me. He died from being stung by bees. I knew he was allergic to them. How do you suppose they got in here, Anna?"

That topic was no better, as far as Anna was concerned. She continued to stare at Tamsin, her face like tragedy's mask. Tamsin was beginning to feel not so much compassionate as exasperated. A girl who had been involved with an "international anarchist" might have a bit more gumption. They could hardly talk about the weather, and Tamsin had decided that it was definitely time to talk. "Did you know Simon had that allergy?" she said.

"He was always careful," Anna muttered. "James used to tease him about it. We felt it was a symbol of his attitude towards the natural world. Bees are so wonderful, so miraculous really. We felt there was something desperately wrong with a person who had to avoid them. Not that I've ever dared to look after the hives myself, but I know that's just me being silly. James always said that if Simon met them with friendship in his heart, and showed them that he was at one with them, they couldn't hurt him. But Simon never had any feeling for the land, or the creatures or anything that genuinely mattered."

"I must say, my own attitude to the countryside has changed since I've lived here," Tamsin said, seizing on a subject which Anna seemed prepared to talk about. "I never used to feel the slightest enthusiasm for the whole-food, noble peasant, earthy life bit. We had lots of friends in London like that, all saving up for their small holdings. I don't want to do without my own modern conveniences, but at least you have shown me that people like you are quite sane."

"We couldn't live any other way. Perhaps we'll be able to get Grebe back now. It's going to be such a wonderful childhood for these two," Anna said. "They must have it."

"You are lucky that James is so stable," Tamsin said.

"Have you heard from your husband again?"

"Yes, he's definitely going to the States. He wants a divorce."

"What will you do?"

"If I ever get out of here?" Tamsin said, and immediately regretted reminding Anna of their situation. She went on quickly, "I don't know quite what to do. I don't know if you'll understand what I mean, but when I got here—as a visitor really—it was hard for me to accept the reality of your sort of life. As a visitor, here, or abroad, anywhere different, one sees other people as almost two-dimensional; nothing bears a relationship to oneself. But now I'm beginning to admire the way you live, people like you and James who have invented a different life, and work and suffer for it. At least, it would be suffering for me, too much like hard work. So I don't see myself living as you do, but I can't imagine going back to the old life in London, either—school runs, dinner parties, marrying another version of Alex in the end, I daresay. I am beginning to feel that I have never lived as myself until this summer—I mean, not in the image of Alex's wife, or my parents' daughter."

"Lucky you, to have been so protected."

"I know. Straight from the arms of my parents to the arms of a husband. But that's over, and not before time. I've got to stand on my own two feet."

"It isn't easy for a mother alone."

"No, but I'll still be luckier than most. Presumably my father and mother would always rally round to pick up the pieces. And I suppose the children will spend some time with Alex. I've never lived all alone. I'm not sure whether I'm looking forward to it, or dreading it."

"It isn't an experience to wish for," Anna said. She got up to shift the sleeping children out of the sun, which was so low in the sky by now as to be coming through the crack of glass which was unobscured. Tamsin tried to make the bunk more comfortable, by pumping up the pillows and shaking out the rug which had been tucked round the mattress. A few dead bees fell out onto the floor.

"I still wonder how the bees got in here," she said. "Do they usually swarm over the sea?"

She thought about the bundle of bees she had seen hanging from the branch of the apple tree, and James waiting to catch it with his wicker skep. A series of pictures flashed through her mind: the skep full of bees, the beekeeper swathing it in cloth and carrying it down to his boat; the silent trip across the water, a cabin door closed on the torpid clump.

Later, hungry bees, starved of pollen; angry bees, without a suitable nook in which to build their hive, their urgent instincts frustrated; a door opens, and a man reeking of the alcohol which enrages them stumbles in through it. He is slowed by being half-drunk, and the door is hard to pull open again on account of the vacuum device which he has put there himself to stop it blowing open at sea.

Would he even have had time to try to escape before he collapsed?

"Would it be murder," Tamsin said slowly, "to expose a man to the substance to which he was allergic?" Then she snapped, "Stop staring at me with those great cow eyes, Anna! If you knew Simon could die from it, did you put a swarm of bees in this cabin? Did you arrange his death?"

"Not me." Anna's lips shaped the words.

"Did James?"

"I don't know."

"I saw James with a swarm of bees."

"I don't know, Tamsin, I don't know."

"But you believe it, don't you? You think he put it in here, knowing that Simon might collapse and die?"

"He threatened our way of life. He threatened the whole environment. Remember about the Blue Butterfly?"

"So James threatened him with nature?"

"He's not a murderer," Anna cried. "If natural creatures killed Simon because he was alien to everything natural—no, Tamsin, no, that wasn't murder!"

"But don't you think it was wrong?" Tamsin protested. "You don't accept nature's verdicts yourself. Emmy would have died when your milk gave out, if nature had been left to decide. Don't you care about what James did?"

"It's easy to make judgements when you have never suffered for them," Anna said. "Easy to be virtuous and moral and live by civilised Western standards. But I have learnt otherwise, ever since my first child came. My responsibility for the world has narrowed down. I'll fight for Emmy and Billy and the life they are to have, and I'll mow down anything that gets in the way of that, anything. Your conscience is a luxury, the luxury of someone who is inexperienced in life."

"But, Anna, what has happened in your life to make you so cruel?"

"I am not cruel," Anna said. Her eyes filled, and water began to roll down and fall off her cheeks. "I'm not cruel. I was brought up to be full of love and compassion. My parents were doctors who looked after the poorest people on earth, the most pitiful, too miserable for you to be able to imagine even. But there wasn't any compassion for my parents, or my brother. There wasn't much for me. When Billy was born I swore that he'd never be so vulnerable. I don't care about anything else anymore, Tamsin, not a soul on earth, nothing except my family. If James protects us, in his own way, I'm glad of it. If Karl and his friends commit their crimes, I'll not open the newspaper that describes them."

"What crimes will they commit?"

"I don't know what they came here for. There will be something they want to blow up. I don't want to think about it."

"Do you mean that they really might use explosives? I thought you meant it metaphorically."

"No, I am not a novelist. I am a realist. I say what I mean. I believe that Karl is making James find his explosives now, because Simon stole them. And then we'll be able to go home. I can't think of that. Can you understand, you perceptive, imaginative writer about the human soul? Do you understand that the only thing that matters is to bring our children to maturity, to keep them safe? You're a mother; you should feel as I do."

"Anna, you said 'explosives.' Do you mean something like dynamite or gelignite?"

"I expect so."

"But Anna! Pippa and Ben are there; the whole class has gone to Grebe today. They might—James might—"

Tamsin battered her fist against the ceiling. "Come down," she shouted. "Whoever you are, come down. Let me out."

"It's Myra," Anna said. "She won't care what you say."

"You are mad, Anna," Tamsin said. "Quite mad." She rattled the door handle and tugged it toward her. Moving heavily against the closing device, the door opened. "There isn't anybody on the roof. Nobody's there," Tamsin said. "Anna, I'm getting out."

CHAPTER 23

The constable who had been sent to relieve Inspector Gemmell, not so much for his sake as because the Superintendent wanted to let his colleague know that several of Karl Fischer's associates had been arrested, crawled through the woods from the inland side so that he would not be seen by anyone on the road. Gemmell did not bother to keep his voice down. With this southwesterly blowing, any sound they made would be carried away from the water. It was hard even to hear the constable's voice, with the soughing of the oak trees and the occasional crack as a dead branch broke off from the trunk.

"Ineffectual lot," the constable said disparagingly. "They wouldn't have done much harm. The first one they found, Ernst something-or-other, gave all the rest away. He was lying up in Plymouth pretending to be a student. They called themselves the New World Liberation Unit."

"I still have the feeling that Karl Fischer is somewhere here," Gemmell said. "I don't see him going off without that kid. If the Buxtons would come back, we might see some action. They can't stay out much longer, surely."

"It's quite rough now, isn't it, sir? Mrs. Oriel wouldn't want to keep that baby on the beach."

"I hate this hot, dry wind. It's like the sirocco or the mistral. Might as well be in the Mediterranean." Gemmell stared at the road and the estuary. Suddenly he put his field glasses to his eyes. "Look, do you see what I see? On the porthole of the *Cock's Comb*, below the tarpaulin. Now that the sun's shining into the cabin, does it look to you as though . . . By God, there is! There's something moving in there. Come on."

The two men went as quickly as was consonant with invisibility down through the woods.

"Take off your jacket, lad. Try to look like a sailor," Gemmell urged. He pointed at a fibreglass pram which was tied on a long rope. "Come on. We'll go in that one. Aim for the red boat further down the river. We'll turn towards the *Cock's Comb* at the last moment."

The two men were pulling steadily across the water when Tamsin emerged from the cabin. They saw the movement, and the constable involuntarily ducked, but she shouted, and they turned their boat towards her, to take the women and the children off.

Grebe had used the same spring since before records began, a bubble of sweet, clear water from deep underground, which was reputed never to have run dry. Certainly even in this year of drought unequalled in the last two centuries, when the reservoirs were revealing long-submerged landmarks, and domestic supplies were soon to be restricted all over southern Britain, the taps at Grebe still let flow a strong gush of water. The well was on the hillside above the farmhouse.

James was exhausted by the time he came to it, not so much from the exertion of searching every conceivable hiding place as from emotional tension. Karl had been needling him all the time, and would not answer James's repeated questions about Anna and the children.

From this vantage point James could see the campers in the field. They sounded happy; they were singing, and in one corner of the field a long table had been erected for meals. James found them as familiar as figures from a well-known picture. They were recognisable, but had no personal connection with him. Over the brow of the hill, in the sand dunes, much higher voices could be heard.

"Hurry up," Karl said. "We don't want to be overrun by a Sunday-school picnic party."

The well was a stone-lined shaft, with a shallow granite sill around it. There was a luxuriant growth of elderberry bushes and other vegetation on the otherwise thirsty hillside.

"You'll have to help me heave this off," James said, gesturing at the heavy planked cover. Together the two men lifted the well cover to one side and stood looking into the round black hole.

"I never knew this place even had a well," Karl said. "Did you have a reason for looking in it?"

"There are alcoves, niches, in the side of the well shaft," James answered.

Karl knelt down to peer in. "Can't see a thing."

James crouched down beside him. "Have you got a torch?" Karl did not answer, but stayed with his head down, trying to accustom his eyes to the darkness. James felt around in the side walls, putting his hands into the recesses in the rock, but pulled out only an ancient earthenware crock with some unidentifiable sediment in it.

"Better see how far the water level's down," he muttered. He fetched a couple of rocks from the hillside.

"What are you doing?" Karl said suspiciously.

"Just checking on the water level. It's an ancient holy well; it hasn't ever been known to run dry. But this summer . . ." He weighed the stone in his hand and walked back to the well.

Myra's head appeared over the brow of the hill. "Karl," she started to shout. "Don't let—"

Karl leapt towards James to grab at his arm, saying sharply, "Don't, it's—"

But the stone had fallen from James's hand.

The level of water had sunk several feet below the package which had been suspended in it. The plastic wrapping around the gun cotton was still mildly moist, because of condensation, and the swathed parcel hung where it had been placed weeks before.

The concussion of the rock which hit it, and the package's disintegration, were virtually simultaneous. The blast of the explosion lifted James Buxton, Karl Fischer and Myra, and several tons of earth and stones, and a great shower of water, and scattered them all over the hillside.

CHAPTER 24

The children who were supposed to be hunting for the Large Blue Butterfly had dispersed in the sand dunes. Mrs. Potter said that they would be perfectly all right so long as they remained in pairs. The boys were playing war games in the natural ramparts and ditches, and the little girls were marking out houses in the hollows, and making dinners of grasses and rabbit droppings. They were all well educated by television; when they heard the noise of the explosion, some dropped flat on the ground like trained guerillas, and the rest waited, frozen like statues, to be told what to do. When they saw the runnels of flame creeping towards them on the ground, they all turned and ran towards the sea.

In the field a tent had been set alight by a floating spark, and the campers wasted several minutes trying to quench the little local fire. As they watched, the flames sprang from the green canvas to the scarlet tent next to it, and the fabric shrivelled away, like a curtain being pulled smoothly back on its cord. At last, much too late, one of the young men leapt to his bicycle and went for help. He pedalled madly up the drive, bouncing over the tarmac rafts.

When they heard the burst of noise, Tamsin was in the dinghy with Inspector Gemmell and the police constable. They were trying to induce Anna to join them in the boat. She was standing on the deck of the *Cock's Comb*, shivering, and gripping Billy's hand, hugging Emmy so tightly to her that the baby's skin bulged out on either side of Anna's arm. They all stared at the Grebe, and the two policemen, experienced and knowing, nodded at one another. Tamsin pushed her hand against the yacht's hull, and shrieked at the men, "Push off! Row! My children are over there!" She fell back on the thwart as the men started to pull towards the shore.

The ground and vegetation were as dry as kindling wood. Warnings had been issued for weeks against inadvertently starting fires in the parched countryside. Flames caught an immediate hold on the Grebe.

By the time that fire engines, attending their ninth call of the day, turned in at the drive, there was little hope of controlling the blaze. The water in the tender was too little to be worth using; the explosion, in destroying the well, had buried the only spring which had not dried up weeks before. On the ebb tide, the sea was far away. The wind acted like a well-managed pair of celestial bellows and fanned every spark into life.

Time passed erratically. Tamsin took a lifetime finding Pippa and Ben. But, safe with their hands in hers, an hour went like a minute, as they watched, beside the other spellbound children, the inexorable advance of the fire. At first they all tried to quench the flames with sand thrown from the children's buckets and spades, even from the butterfly nets and their bare hands. Some of the children had fetched pailfuls of seawater. But the fire advanced through the dunes like the sea itself, in waves which sometimes seemed to be retreating but always moved their tide mark, eventually, in its destined direction. In some places the flames were bushes blossoming on the tips of the long grass, elsewhere almost invisible points of light near the ground. Promontories jutted forward from the main area of the fire; elsewhere smooth and gentle eddies of bluish flames separated the blackened ground from the still unscorched sand.

On the landward side of the fire's centre the outbreak seemed more controllable at first. The party of campers at last realised what they should have been doing already, and made enthusiastic swipes with brooms and shovels, blankets and empty rucksacks, against the flames. At one moment they thought that the fire was contained within a ring of their energy, but then one of the girls saw that the ground behind her was smouldering, and that over the wall the leaves on one of the apple trees were blackening and shrivelling before her eyes. When the professional fire-fighters arrived the campers were surrounded by patches of fire, but still fought desperately, like commando troops, with blackened faces and hands.

Inspector Gemmell appropriated one of the newspaper reporter's cars and went to the neighbouring farm to set Leonard Hosking and his men to ploughing a strip of land between his fields and the Grebe. Gemmell watched for a little while as the men drove their tractors over the precious shoots of green, churning the earth over every ignitable fragment.

Smoke gusted inland on the fierce wind. The fire was reaching the boundary of the headland, within which the firemen were trying to contain the unquenchable blaze. From time to time grimy figures lurched out of the fog, mopping at their faces and gasping. Gemmell made his way down the field. He went past two calm naturalists who were leaning against the stone wall beside which the farm workmen had dug their firebreak. They had notebooks and cameras and were charting the lists of refugees. Gemmell had noticed several rabbits himself, as they dashed across his path. These men had listed many varieties of small animals which were escaping from the conflagration, and even more of birds. They seemed less dismayed by the habitat's destruction than excited by what they were seeing, as lizards and adders, voles and shrews emerged from their secret places. Those which got away in time, they said, would be a tiny proportion of the wildlife which would perish.

"Not much chance of containing the fire now," one said.

"I should think the whole headland has had it. It's a tragedy," the other replied.

They were quite right; the official and voluntary fire-fighters laboured on for the rest of the evening and most of the night. By the very early morning it seemed certain that Leonard Hosking's land was saved, but that nothing on the Grebe would escape. The campers stayed to help, though the firemen found them a hindrance. The school-children were taken off in dinghies from the beach. Tamsin was with them, and as they rowed up the river past the silent *Cock's Comb* she saw one of the stunted oak trees under which she had lain with Simon Wherry flash into an incandescent torch.

The fire had been fiercest near its source. When it finally became possible to explore the ruined farm, the remains of three bodies were found on the hillside above the orchard, their calcined bones capriciously revealed beside undamaged flesh, nakedness beside tatters of fabric, smooth hair beside shrivelled wiry clumps.

Gemmell went to River House the day after the fire started; it was still burning, but under a kind of control. Anna was milking the goat, and the children playing in the field. He was used to the policeman's sad task of announcing death.

"I know," Anna said. "I know."

"That your husband is dead?"

"Both of them," she answered. "Both dead."

Gemmell did not feel equal to bringing up the subject of legal divorce, or false statements on passport application forms, still less to discussing allergic reactions to bee stings. He asked Anna to give him the passport in the name of Mrs. Buxton, and reminded her that a close watch was being kept now, and would always be kept in future, on entrants to the small ports and harbours. Gemmell knew by now, but did not mention, that there was evidence that James, not Anna, had placed the skep of bees in the *Cock's Comb* cabin. He had been seen with the swathed package in his dinghy by an old man who said he could have told the police that weeks ago if he'd known they were interested.

The headland blazed all that day, and all the day after; for weeks it continued to smoulder; the ground was hot, and trickles of smoke rose between the blackened charcoal sticks which had been clumps of heather and the charred stones now falling from the walls. Sometimes a clump of marram grass which had survived would ignite, from the fire which travelled along its roots under the sand. On the dark ground the white of seagulls gleamed, and old tin cans, and fragments of broken glass, and snail shells. The fresh green of bracken began to show in patches on the powdery soil even before the fire was completely out, but the other vegetation, including the rare thyme which was a necessary part of the Large Blue Butterfly's reproductive cycle, would not revive for years, if ever.

CHAPTER 25

Tamsin was sickened by the persistent smell of smoke and her awareness of tragedy. She moved herself and the children out of the cottage, realising as she did so that she was deplorably avoiding the contagion of grief. They went to the south of France, where it rained, and read about the continuing drought in England. As Tamsin returned painlessly and unchallenged through the passport controls, she thought, confusedly, about fairness, and luck, and oppression. The three of them went straight from the holiday to London, where the local police, always cooperative to solid citizens, helped Tamsin to break into her own house, of which she had lost the key.

Alex had been away for some time. There was a heap of junk mail and some unforwarded letters to Tamsin on the mat. The children were delighted to see their own rooms and own toys after so long; the police constable was charming and helped Tamsin to light the gas boiler, and disposed of some spiders in the downstairs cloakroom and a dead mouse in the larder without mentioning them to Tamsin.

The Oriels had baked beans for supper, because they were the only tins which Alex had left uneaten. Tamsin threw away some alien cosmetics which she found on her dressing table, and some strange medicines in the bathroom cabinet, but she decided to keep and wear a pretty silk headscarf which must have been chosen to go with Clarissa's colouring. In the morning, she decided, she would telephone the oil headquarters and get Alex's address; she would go to the hairdresser and call on her agent; she might even start writing a new book.

Even before Tamsin went off to France, Sir Arnold and

Lady Lurie had taken charge of Anna's affairs. "The poor child can't possibly manage," they told each other. Sir Arnold used the power of his personality and experience to stall his former colleagues in their probing of Anna's past. He used his tact and diplomacy and prestige to smooth things over with the Withiel police; he persuaded the priest in charge of Withiel's Catholic Church to hold a ceremony over James's un-Catholic corpse, and assured Anna that in the eyes of God it would not matter whose widow men said she was.

After a while he decided that Anna could not live on a precipice overhanging a thicket of criminal charges and deportation orders. He was the better poacher for having been so high-powered a gamekeeper, and managed, not directly but by implication, to get one of the boys from the aborted commune at Grebe to offer to lend Anna his nationality. They went through the ceremony of marriage at the registry office where Anna had previously, bigamously, done so with James. The young man then accepted his reward and set off at once on the golden route overland to the places, not very far from Anna's original home, where he hoped to find truth, peace, and an unlimited supply of hallucinogenic drugs. Protected by the nationality he had thus conferred on her, Anna was better able to face the prospect of punishment without banishment for her undoubted offences against administrative laws. But no charges were preferred against her; after several months, she was informally told that the matters would not be pursued.

The resumed inquest on Simon Wherry found that his death had been manslaughter at the hands of James Buxton, whose own death was attributed to accident.

Under Granny Wherry's will, James would, as he always knew, have inherited the Grebe, but he did not survive Simon for the period specified in Granny's will and Simon's sister in America became the owner of an estate not only encumbered with heavy duties but ruined for years to come. She sold it through the solicitors, without coming home, to a company which operated holiday camps. Now that there was little to conserve, they received permission easily to build two hundred permanent letting units, operate a camp for tourist tents and caravans, and build a swimming pool, clubhouse, restaurant and bar.

Anna found her art gallery too much to cope with on her own. She closed it down, repaying the Arts Council's grant. When Emmy started going to the playgroup, to which she was admitted young as a child in a "one-parent family," Anna took a job behind the bar at the Grebe holiday camp.

Tamsin found her there when she came down to Cornwall the following April, a year after she had first met Simon Wherry.

"I've got a contract to write the affair up for a colour supplement," she explained.

"Your parents told me you were coming." Anna had got into the habit of taking Billy and Emmy to lunch with the Luries at weekends; her children called Sir Arnold and Lady Lurie "Grandad and Grandma"; there were supplies of toys kept for them in the bungalow in Brannell, and Anna accepted the Luries' advice about Billy's behaviour problems. Sir Arnold had pulled some other strings and arranged for Billy to be taken before he was five at the primary school.

"You are giving them an interest," Tamsin said. She had been disconcerted, on arriving at her parents' house, to find so little evidence of herself, Pippa and Ben, and so much of Anna, Billy and Emmy.

"It sounds as though you have found other interests for yourself," Anna remarked. She had tried, unsuccessfully, to get the Luries to persuade Tamsin to refuse the commission to write up last year's events.

"Journalism is terrific fun. Much more interesting than novels. Look at your own life, for instance, completely implausible from start to finish. Look at you now. If you were a fictional heroine, I wouldn't have dared to make you end up serving drinks to tourists in a bar full of fake helms and lanterns and ships' instruments."

Some visitors entered the bar, and Anna drew their pints with a practised pressure on the handle.

"I've changed as far as that goes," she said. "But only because it lets me stick to my original priority."

"I suppose the money helps too."

The money helped, little as it was, insofar as it made Anna seem independent to the curious world. She was free for life, with her secret nest egg, or dowry, from the interference and assistance of clerks or welfare workers. She didn't want people to wonder where her money came from, though. Later in the year she would take in paying guests at River House, and the cottage was already fully booked for holiday lets.

"I think I have the facts straight now," Tamsin said, getting out her notebook. "My difficulty is with motives. It all seems so unlike James, as I knew him, for instance. My mother says you don't mind talking about him."

"Whatever you say about him, he wasn't a murderer. If you have to write this, at least make that clear. He was leaving it to nature, or fate, whatever you call it. Simon needn't have been killed by the bees. If he'd been sober when he went into the cabin . . . It was his own fault in a way; he brought it on himself."

"James must have wondered what was going on when nothing happened. No Simon, no body, the *Cock's Comb* still there . . . What's happened to the boat, by the way?"

"It was sold. The new owner is a member here."

"And, Anna, Karl Fischer—did he really think he could change the world? Do you know?"

"He believed that was how the world gets changed, I think."

"But so inefficient. I mean, the gun cotton, for instance, that was put in the well—it seems that nobody uses that nowadays; they use plastic explosives. If only they had used those . . ."

"They did have plastic explosives, for the letter bombs. But their main plan depended on an explosive that went off on impact, that and the remote-control device. Myra knew her stuff, oddly enough. She'd been to a course for terrorists, in Morocco."

"It sounds miserably ineffective."

"Well, Tamsin," Anna said, rubbing the cloth round and round the rim of a beer tankard, "they were ineffective. That was the whole point. Karl could never have hit his real targets, only the innocent people who got in his line of fire. Your father says he was the most dangerous kind of enthusiast, the one with a bad aim. But he tried, I suppose. What else was there for him to do?"

Tamsin made some notes on her pad. "What do you think of this?" she said. " 'Both rejected the exploitative and parasitic characteristics of modern society; Karl, frustrated by social handicaps, wanted a social revolution, but he had never gone so far as to decide what he would put in the place of the world he wished to destroy. James opted out, and hoped to create a new life-style in which human, social and ecological concerns would be harmoniously woven together.' "

"I am sorry," Anna interrupted. "I can't listen to that kind of thing."

"Oh, Anna, I'm awfully sorry. I didn't think—"

"It isn't the matter; it's the jargon. James had perfectly simple motives; he wanted to leave other people alone and be left alone, and he suffered for not sticking to his principles. As for Karl—he hadn't had a safe and beloved childhood. He'd never learnt to care about other people. That was the real difference between him and James. Karl would kill for the sake of ideas, like Western man throughout history. James had ideas, but he wouldn't even kill animals for them. And he died because he didn't stick to his principles."

Two men came into the bar, and ordered pink gin and whisky. Anna poured carefully, with the deliberate skill she had once applied to arranging pictures and sculptures.

One of the newcomers was the man whom Tamsin had once seen at a private-view party in Anna's gallery; the one who boasted about his weekend trips on his powerful cruiser. He was talking about his new yacht.

"Got her cheap. There was a death on board."

"Will you change her name?"

"Yes, I'm not superstitious. We've christened her *Chicken Licken*."

"Got a lot to do to her?"

"She's not in bad nick, considering. I've been down checking the mooring this morning, making sure the chain and weight are all right. Look what I found fastened to one of the submerged links. What do you think it is?"

He held up a small, smooth, black box, with a retractable aerial. "It was all wrapped up, inside a sealed box. Must have been lying on the seabed."

"Looks like some sort of radio."

"No, it's more like one of those model-aeroplane doo-dahs."

Anna spoke clearly. "That," she said, "is a remote-controlled detonating device." She took it from the man's hand and set it on the fake pinewood of the bar counter, beside a ship's compass which had never been afloat and a sea-urchin shell. It looked almost at home, surrounded by fronds of plastic seaweed, in its artificial nautical display.

About the Author

Jessica Mann was educated at Cambridge, where she studied archaeology and Anglo-Saxon. She is the author of eight other books, and is also a respected critic for *British Book News* and the BBC. She lives with her husband and four children in Cornwall. *The Sting of Death* is her second novel for the Crime Club.